W9-BOS-671

WINDOWS ON THE HILL

Crown Point Community Library
214 South Court Street
Crown Point, Indiana   46307

DISCARDED

Books by Beverly Lewis

GIRLS ONLY (GO!)
Youth Fiction

Dreams on Ice	Follow the Dream
Only the Best	Better Than Best
A Perfect Match	Photo Perfect
Reach for the Stars	Star Status

SUMMERHILL SECRETS
Youth Fiction

Whispers Down the Lane	House of Secrets
Secret in the Willows	Echoes in the Wind
Catch a Falling Star	Hide Behind the Moon
Night of the Fireflies	Windows on the Hill
A Cry in the Dark	Shadows Beyond the Gate

HOLLY'S HEART
Youth Fiction

Best Friend, Worst Enemy	Straight-A Teacher
Secret Summer Dreams	No Guys Pact
Sealed With a Kiss	Little White Lies
The Trouble With Weddings	Freshman Frenzy
California Crazy	Mystery Letters
Second-Best Friend	Eight Is Enough
Good-Bye, Dressel Hills	It's a Girl Thing

WINDOWS ON THE HILL

Beverly Lewis

BETHANY HOUSE PUBLISHERS
MINNEAPOLIS, MINNESOTA 55438

Windows On the Hill
Copyright © 1999
Beverly Lewis

Cover illustration by Chris Ellison
Cover design by the Lookout Design Group

All rights reserved. No part of this publication may be reproduced,
stored in a retrieval system, or transmitted in any form or by any
means—electronic, mechanical, photocopying, recording, or
otherwise—without the prior written permission of the publisher
and copyright owners.

Published by Bethany House Publishers
11400 Hampshire Avenue South
Bloomington, Minnesota 55438
www.bethanyhouse.com

Bethany House Publishers is a Division of
Baker Book House Company, Grand Rapids, Michigan.

Printed in the United States of America

ISBN 1-55661-875-1 (pbk.)

For
Julie Witner,
who loves cats as much as
Merry Hanson.

BEVERLY LEWIS is a speaker, teacher, and the best-selling author of the HOLLY'S HEART series. She has written over fifty books for adults, teens, and children. Many of her articles and stories have appeared in the nation's top magazines.

Beverly is a member of the National League of American Pen Women and the Society of Children's Book Writers and Illustrators. She and her husband, Dave, along with their three teenagers, live in Colorado. She fondly remembers their cockapoo named Cuddles, who used to snore to Mozart!

"For the eyes of the Lord run to and fro throughout the whole earth . . ."

—II Chronicles 16:9 KJV

ONE

I'll never forget the day my sweet and sassy Abednego disappeared. The afternoon was unseasonably warm and sultry. Too warm for the middle of April.

Perched on the garden bench under our backyard maple, I played with the lens cap on my best camera. I'd loaded it with oodles of film for today's special event—a retirement party for my dad. Actually, the party was an open house, a come-and-go sort of thing. I wouldn't have admitted it, but I was truly bored out of my mind.

My cat quartet—Shadrach, Meshach, Abednego, and Lily White—gathered around my feet. I figured they were horribly hot and uncomfortable inside their heavy fur coats. Fidgety, they rolled around in the cool grass, pawing at one another.

I leaned back and gazed up at the pale blue sky. A series of ballooning white clouds sped across the heavens. Mom liked to call them thunderheads. I nicknamed them thunderbumpers.

"Looks like rain," I told my feline friends. "Those clouds up there are gonna crash together and make all kinds of racket pretty soon." I didn't realize that what I'd just said would actually happen. And in a very frightening way.

The cats didn't seem too alarmed by my comment. Only Abednego lifted his fat, furry head and stared at me. His eyes blinked slowly: one . . . two . . . three. Then he put his head down again and licked his paws.

"What's on your mind, little boy?" I reached down for him, but he hissed back at me. "Abednego! Is that any way to behave?"

He responded by making a beeline for the gazebo, squeezing his plump black belly under the white lattice-work—his favorite hiding spot. Whenever he was missing, I first checked under the gazebo.

"He's upset about something," I muttered, playing with Lily White, my fluffy white kitten. Sitting there, I felt a bit miffed at Abednego, not knowing what on earth was on his mind. I also felt somewhat indifferent toward the strangers in our yard. Several former colleagues of Dad's had already arrived—emergency room nurses and doctors. They were laughing and sharing stories in the shelter of the large gazebo.

Originally, Mom had decided to book a downtown hotel suite for the occasion. In the end, though, Dad got his way—a simple springtime picnic on the grounds of our one-hundred-year-old farmhouse.

Casually, I looked toward the back porch and noticed

Mom motioning from the kitchen window. She called through the screen. "Merry, come and help serve finger food."

I was glad she'd asked—something to do. Quickly, I left my private post, and the three remaining cats insisted on following me up the back steps and into the house.

By the time I arrived in the kitchen, Mom was occupied with the arrangement of carrot sticks, celery, raw cauliflower, and broccoli on one side of a round tray.

When I caught her eye, I noticed she seemed a bit stressed. "Please pass this tray around outside, honey." She glanced at the sky through the wide kitchen window. "And pray that the weather holds."

Her request was understandable. With temperatures soaring and humidity hovering in the ninety percent range, the chance of a storm was extremely high. I hoped—and prayed—for both Dad's and Mom's sake that the breeze might blow the ominous clouds far away.

I headed toward the back door carrying the enormous tray. My mouth watered at the sight of the creamy, homemade buttermilk dressing smack-dab in the center. There were other delicacies, too, and I made note of the barbecued chicken wings and drumsticks, hoping some of them might get passed over so I could have a taste later.

Dad's party was in full swing. The gazebo was filling

up with folks offering their best wishes for his early retirement. Gingerly, I carried the tray across the yard and up the white wooden gazebo steps.

"Here's my girl," Dad said. His eyes lit up as he began making introductions. "This is my daughter, Merry. She's quite the photographer, so you may see her roaming the grounds taking nonposed shots."

"Hello. Nice to meet you," I said, smiling and feeling terribly awkward, yet offering my absolute courtesy.

Dad nodded, obviously pleased that I'd made an attempt to chat. "Merry's making a scrapbook of the afternoon," he commented. "So her old dad will remember this day."

"Oh, Daddy," I said, feeling the heat of embarrassment work its way into my face. "You're not old."

Several of the men agreed.

"My daughter's an optimistic young lady," Dad said, winking at me.

"And she must be very thoughtful, too," added one of the nurses, smiling. She went on to say that she'd attended a creative workshop on scrapbooking recently. "What a wonderful way to record special memories."

She's right about that, I thought, recalling the cherished scrapbooks of my twin sister, Faithie, and me. The long-ago pictures brought back some of the happiest days of my life—snapped photos taken before Faithie died of leukemia at age seven.

I kept smiling and playing hostess, taking the tray items around to fifteen or more people. The finger food vanished quickly, and I headed toward the house to stock up.

"Merry, honey," Dad called. "Why don't we have a group picture when you come back out?"

"Okay," I replied and hurried into the kitchen.

"Back so soon?" Mom said, eyeing the empty tray.

I nodded. "People are showing up in droves. Probably because of all the free food."

"Merry, for goodness' sake," Mom scolded. "Your father's a highly respected doctor in Lancaster County."

"*Was* . . ."

She was shaking her head at me. "C'mon, Merry. You know what I mean."

"Sorry, Mom. It just came out wrong."

She fell silent, going about the business of scraping more carrots. I leaned against the fridge, watching Lily White chase her golden-haired brothers around the corner and into the family room.

"Are the Zooks coming?" I asked, thinking of our Amish neighbors and good friends.

Mom answered without looking up. "Abe and Esther and the children were invited. I'd be very surprised if they didn't drop in for a while."

"What about Old Hawk Eyes? Do you think *she'll* come?"

Mom's head jerked up. Her deep brown eyes bored into me. "Merry, now, really."

I wrinkled my nose. "Everyone calls Miss Spindler

that . . . even the Zook kids!"

Mom shook her head. "Does she deserve a nickname like that?"

"Well, she's always spying on the neighborhood. Always seems to know exactly what's going on in SummerHill, you know."

Mom knew it was true, but she had too many things on her mind to argue with me now. "Ruby Spindler is a lonely old lady, but she has a heart of gold" was all she said.

I bit my tongue—wasn't going to remind Mom unduly of Miss Spindler's nosy behavior. I headed back outside to prepare for the group picture Dad wanted. That's when a crack of thunder like I'd never heard boomed down on the party.

Abednego darted out from under the gazebo as though he'd been shot. He came straight for me across the yard, and if I hadn't stood perfectly still he would've tangled up in my feet and made me fall, camera and all.

Another deafening thunderclap followed, and I ran to the safety of the house. Inside, I set down my camera equipment and raced to the family room windows, hoping to see where my elderly cat had run for cover.

Then I spotted him. His long black tail was pointing straight up as he dashed around the side of the house, heading for the road.

"Yee-ikes!" I said, hurrying back to the kitchen.

"What is it, dear?" Mom asked, scurrying about.

"I think Abednego's completely flipped out." I didn't bother to explain. But I had the strangest feeling that I might never see my beloved baby again.

TWO

I scrambled to the hall closet and pulled out an old raincoat and hat. Those thunderbumpers had done their job, given clear warning. The sky opened right up like a burst dam.

My golden-haired cats—Shadrach and Meshach—and Lily White at least had enough sense to come in out of the storm. They'd made a beeline to the stairs that led to my bedroom. Actually, it was sort of *their* room, too, since I allowed all four of my cats to sleep at the foot of my big bed.

Now, standing by the front door, I snapped up my waterproof coat and hat, wondering where to look for Abednego. How could I persuade my old cat to come home?

People poured into the kitchen, located at the back of the house. I could hear Mom's voice mixed in with the swell of animated conversation; the casual comments about it "pouring cats and dogs." The only problem was one of *my* cats was getting drenched out there. And the poor thing was way too old and feeble to survive getting caught in this sort of gully washer.

Without telling Mom or anyone, I ducked my head and ran out into the drenching rain. Rain pellets fell so hard they were like tiny hammers on my rain hat.

"Abednego!" I hollered.

The rain was roaring, coming straight down in fierce sheets. I retraced his steps and dashed back to the gazebo, squatted down, and looked under the latticework, hoping . . . hoping he might've run back here to hide.

"Here, kitty, kitty," I called again and again.

Standing there like a statue in the rain and wind, I wondered which direction to take, thinking he might've headed up Strawberry Lane—the road that ran along the north side of our property. Miss Spindler lived up that road, and Abednego might've gone there to find refuge under the thicket and large trees surrounding her old house.

I hurried across the backyard to Strawberry Lane, leaning my head into the wind. Looking down, I noticed that I'd forgotten to wear rain boots, and my sneakers were soaked and muddy. Nevertheless, I pushed on, arriving at Miss Spindler's stately residence.

I rang the doorbell, and she came quickly, her blue-gray hair and makeup absolutely perfect, as always. In fact, if I wasn't mistaken, it looked as if she'd had her hair dyed a shade of cobalt blue. Politely, I squelched a giggle.

"My, oh my, what're you doin' out in this, dearie?"

she greeted me. "Goodness me, Merry, you're soakin' wet."

"It's my cat," I blubbered. "Abednego's run off. Have you seen him?"

She shook her head slowly. "There ain't been no sign of man nor beast since this terrible storm came up. But I'll be on the lookout for him," she assured me.

I wondered what she meant by "on the lookout." Maybe she really did have a lookout room somewhere in the house. Was *that* how she spied on everyone and everything?

"Well, thank you, Miss Spindler. I better keep searching for my cat."

She clucked her tongue at me, as if to say I shouldn't be out in such inclement weather, but I couldn't let her discourage me.

"We're gonna have us a good time when you come next week," she said through the screen door.

I smiled at her. "Yes, I'm looking forward to it." Which was actually a true statement. I simply *had* to find that lookout room of hers!

Stumbling back down Strawberry Lane, I made the turn onto SummerHill Lane at the bottom of the hill. There I scanned the ditches on either side of the road. Tears stung my eyes as I thought of losing my cat to this vicious storm.

With renewed determination, I trudged onward, toward our Amish neighbor's private lane. Where was Abednego? Had he gone for shelter in the Zooks' barn?

Bowed against the ferocious gale, I might've wandered into the path of the oncoming Amish buggy, but the horse neighed loudly enough to penetrate the sound of the pounding rain. Heart thumping, I stopped dead in my tracks.

Not more than a few yards away, Ol' Apple—one of Abe Zook's driving horses—was snorting and stomping and rearing his head. Slowly, I backed away, hoping to calm him so he wouldn't tip over the carriage. "It's just me . . . Merry Hanson," I said, even though I couldn't imagine the horse even heard my voice. Still, I moved back gradually till I sensed he was beginning to relax.

Then I heard Abe Zook speaking to his horse in a monotone Pennsylvania Dutch—gentle and composed.

I'm not sure how long I stood there, but I was shivering, that much I knew. My teeth began to chatter, more from the near accident than from the cold.

"Merry, *kumm mit!*" Abe Zook called. "Come along into the buggy. We'll take ya home."

"Thank you!" I was glad for the invitation but still concerned about Abednego. Yet as I settled into the second seat, next to my Plain girl friend, Rachel, I didn't say a word about my runaway pet.

"We're headed over to your pop's retirement party," Rachel said. Her pretty blue eyes glimmered with expectancy.

"It's not such a good day for it, I'm afraid," I said as the carriage creaked and struggled up the muddy hill.

"*Jah*, but it'll pass," she said, smiling. "Bad weather always does."

Her positive, upbeat attitude always left me nearly breathless. The climate outside or inside really didn't matter—the oldest daughter of our Old Order Amish neighbors was usually on top of the world, so to speak.

"What're you doin' out in this rain?" asked Esther from the front seat.

I hesitated to mention my foolish cat. "Well, did you hear those thunderclaps?" I ventured.

They nodded that they had . . . all the kids, too.

"My cat took off running right after that," I said.

"Which cat?" asked seven-year-old Susie, the youngest.

"Abednego, the oldest."

"Ain't he the one always runnin' off?" asked Aaron, the youngest boy.

"Always," I answered.

"Best do something 'bout that," Ella Mae, age nine, spoke up.

"Like what?" asked her older sister Nancy.

"Maybe get him a cage," giggled Susie.

Rachel shushed her. "Now, don't make fun," she said.

I was thankful for my friend's comment. After all, my precious cat was still wandering around out in this nasty weather. Lost!

"Heard you was stayin' over at Old Hawk Eyes' a bit next week," Rachel whispered. "While your parents go on a trip."

"Just three days . . . till my brother gets home from college for his Easter break," I explained.

Susie and Ella Mae were leaning up behind us, their noses poking over the seat where Rachel and I sat. "Why ain'tcha comin' to stay with us?" asked Ella Mae.

"Well, Mom talked about asking you, but then she decided your mama has enough children to keep track of." I wanted to admit that I'd much rather spend three days at their Amish dairy farm than stay with Miss Spindler at all.

Still, there was something I was dying to find out. There was a secret waiting inside Old Hawk Eyes' house, probably in her attic. Only I hadn't told a soul.

At least, not yet . . .

THREE

The guests who came to help Dad celebrate were either Plain or fancy—the phrase used here in Pennsylvania to describe the difference between Amish or Mennonite folk and regular modern people like me and my family.

I took plenty of pictures indoors—for the retirement scrapbook. In spite of the rainstorm, my father's former colleagues continued to show up in groups of three or four. None of the medical types were Plain, though. They were highly educated people, unlike the Amish, who abandoned formal schooling after the eighth grade. Higher learning was strongly discouraged by Amish bishops. They believed that if a person searched for knowledge and found it, the risk of straying from the path of the *Ordnung*—the unwritten rules of the Amish community—was too high to keep him in the Old Order.

Dad and I went around the house together—arm in arm—introducing our Amish neighbors, the Abe Zook family, including their homegrown children: Rachel, Nancy, Aaron, Ella Mae, and little Susie.

Levi, their next-to-oldest son, was off in Virginia at a Mennonite college, finding his way in the world of cars and electricity. And Curly John, the Zooks' firstborn, had already settled down to marriage with his young bride, Sarah.

Abe and Esther Zook didn't waste any time locating my mother after introductions were finished. They strolled from the living room right out to the kitchen and made themselves at home.

But Rachel hung back with me, and we found a spot in the family room to chat a bit. "What's your pop gonna do with himself since he ain't workin' no more?" she came right out and asked. Her fingers slid up and down the white strings on her *kapp*—the head covering she always wore.

I knew the answer to that question. "My dad wants to take a few mission trips overseas, going as a helper to construction missionaries. I think he'll keep plenty busy, especially with building churches and Bible schools. That's what he likes best."

"Well, if there's any time when he's twiddling his thumbs, you just send him on over to *Dat*. He'll put him to *gut* use in a hurry." Rachel's rosy face shone under the lamp behind the chair.

I laughed but not too hard. Growing up around Amish helped me understand these good-hearted people. "Sure, I'll tell him. But it wouldn't hurt for your father to do the same, probably."

"Right ya be," Rachel said, smoothing her long blue dress.

Rachel and her sisters were grinning hard at me. I couldn't resist. I had to know what was on their minds. "What's up?" I asked.

They glanced back and forth at one another as they sat on the sofa, like they were too shy to say.

"C'mon, I know you've got something up your sleeves," I urged.

Rachel finally spoke up. "I probably shouldn't say nothing, what with Abednego acting up and all."

I hadn't forgotten my lost cat, not for a single second. But her remark hit home, and I excused myself and got up to look out the window. *Where are you, Abednego?* I wondered.

"We've got us too many kittens," Rachel said, almost abruptly.

Her words hardly registered in my brain. Sadly, I turned away from the window. "What did you say?"

"We got us more cats than we know what to do with," repeated Ella Mae.

Nancy was nodding her head to beat the band. "Dat's gonna hafta shoot 'em if we don't find 'em homes," she said.

"Aw, you're not serious. Would he do that, really?" I shouldn't have asked because I knew Abe was more than eager to lessen the cat population on his dairy farm. Cats had a tendency to get in the way—made farm work difficult, getting all tangled up underfoot.

"I think kitty cats are awful cute," little Susie piped up. "Can't ya take a couple more?"

I shook my head. "My mother's upset about the four cats I already have. She'd never stand for five!"

"*Ach*, what's the difference?" Rachel asked. "Four, five, or twenty—they're all just cats. Makes for good mouse catchin'."

Thinking about that, I realized we hadn't seen a single mouse in over a year. "You're probably right."

"So . . . do ya want another one, then?" Rachel asked, grinning from ear to ear.

I shook my head and sat down again. "Better not even ask my mother. She might drop that big tray of goodies over there." Through the wide doorway, we watched her pick her way through the growing *indoor* crowd of well-wishers.

"Won't it seem funny havin' your pop home all the time?" Rachel asked. Her light brown hair was parted simply down the middle, but specks of light danced prettily on the sides.

"When Dad's home, he'll keep busy with hobbies and volunteer work at the hospital and the church. And there's always my mother's growing fascination with antiques," I explained.

"Your *Mam* likes old furniture?" Rachel asked while her sisters were silent, just smiling.

"She's smitten with antique fever. Next thing I know, she'll be starting up a shop somewhere in this house." I glanced outside at the gazebo. "I wouldn't be surprised at anything."

Rachel pushed the hairs at her neck up into her bun, under the thin white netting. "So . . . you're sure you don't need another cat or two?"

"Not if I want to keep living here," I said, laughing.

"Okay, then. I won't bring it up again." She got up and went to the kitchen with me to get a plate and some finger food. Her sisters followed right along without ever saying a word.

"Wait a minute." I just thought of someone who might be in the market for a kitten. "Have you talked to Miss Spindler? She'd be a good cat person, I think."

Rachel's eyes lit up. "Are ya sure?"

"One-hundred-percent-amen sure!" I said.

"Jah . . . Old Hawk Eyes *does* need a cat," Nancy said out of the blue.

"She must be awful lonely over there in that great big house of hers, don'tcha think so, Rachel?" asked Ella Mae.

I smiled. "Nancy and Ella Mae are probably right." Just then Shadrach and Meshach scampered into the room. "Excuse me," I said quickly. "I'd better round up my cats before Mom says they're spoiling Dad's party."

"Need any help?" asked Rachel.

"Sure!"

So we ran around the family room, finally catching up with Abednego's little brothers. It was usually the feisty, fat feline I was chasing. Shadrach and Meshach weren't nearly as adventuresome these days. The farthest they'd ever strayed was the willow grove, the dividing line between the Zooks' property and ours.

But Abednego was another story. He'd been known to wander off as far away as the highway, clear to the east end of SummerHill Lane. I didn't want to think about my cat running away today. Not with the rain continuing to pour down in buckets.

But I had to admit, I was worried something awful about Abednego being gone this long. Truly worried!

FOUR

I don't happen to swallow all that stuff about cats having nine lives. People get carried away with notions sometimes, I think. But if the nine-lives thing were really true, I guess I'd have had higher hopes of Abednego's return.

Yet I continued to stare out my second-floor window into the twilight, missing my fat black cat. My deep affection for him kept me standing there, motionless, remembering all the years spent with the spunkiest cat in all of SummerHill.

Finally I forced myself away from the rain-streaked window. It wasn't that I was giving up on finding him. The night was just so wet and cold. Too blustery to go searching the countryside again. Even Mom had put her foot down about my going back out.

But I had a plan. A pure genius strategy to help locate Abednego. I sat at my desk with pen and paper, beginning to outline my idea.

Soon I was lost in a world of alliterated words when

someone knocked softly on my bedroom door. "Say the secret slogan," I said.

Dad peeked his head in. "Hey, honeybunch."

"That's not a password," I replied.

"Close?" He shrugged and cocked his head to one side.

"Not even."

"Okay, I give up," he said, offering a winning smile. "May I come in?"

I sighed. "For you, no password required."

Opening the door wider, he moseyed inside. He stood near my antique dresser, frowning cautiously. "How're you doing, kiddo?"

Quickly, I looked away.

"You're upset," he said, coming over.

"Abednego's disappeared," I blurted. "I'm worried sick."

"Of course you are, honey. Your cats mean a lot to you."

Shadrach, Meshach, and Lily White perked up and looked at Dad as if they'd heard their own names. I had to smile, wondering what went through those furry little heads at a time like this. With Big Brother lost in the night somewhere.

Dad stood in the middle of the room, eyes soft and gentle. For a moment I thought I saw them glisten. "I wanted to come up and say thanks for helping your mother this afternoon. And for taking all those indoor pictures."

I felt almost shy. "It was a great retirement party, Dad. I was glad to help out."

He shook his head, then sat at the foot of my bed. "I'm having second thoughts."

"About retirement?"

That got a chuckle. "No . . . no, not at all. This old man's eager and ready for a change of pace."

"And scenery, too?" I added quickly, thinking of my parents' Costa Rica trip.

He looked at me with compassionate eyes. "I'm wondering if leaving you with Miss Spindler is the right thing," he began again. "Maybe we should postpone the trip until this summer and go together, as a family."

"I'll be fine, Dad. Miss Spindler's looking forward to having someone around. I'll keep her company."

He nodded as if reevaluating the idea. "And you'll be there only a short time," he admitted.

"Three days." *Enough time to do some snooping*, I thought.

"Then it's settled," he said. "When your brother arrives home, he'll look after you until we return."

I went to him and offered a hug. "I'm not a child anymore, Dad. You don't have to worry."

He got up and walked to the door, smiling. "Well, I'm glad we had this little talk."

"Me too. Old Hawk Eyes and I will get along okay."

That's when he laughed so loud Mom came and poked her head in the room, too. I didn't feel the need to rehearse the "Old Hawk Eyes" issue again.

"What's so funny?" She leaned against the door frame.

I glanced at Dad, deciding it was up to him to tell her. He was cool that way—truly understood the need for appropriate nicknames.

The phone rang, and I was more than happy to excuse myself, speeding down the hall to get it.

"Hanson residence," I answered. "Merry speaking."

"Merry *speaking*? When did you change your name?"

I laughed. "Oh, it's *you*."

"So how's the feline freak?" Skip asked.

I could almost visualize my older brother's straight face. He wasn't joking, not one bit. Honestly, he believed that I was cat crazy.

"You'll probably be glad to hear that I'm short one cat at the moment," I informed him.

"Well, that *is* good news." He chortled a bit, then continued. "Let me guess . . . Abednego got run over by an Amish buggy."

"Skip Hanson!"

"Hey . . . just kidding. But it *is* Abednego who's missing, right?"

"You know my cats pretty well," I said but didn't want to continue this line of conversation. "So . . ." I paused. "Why'd you really call?"

"Just checking up on my little Merry" came the saucy reply.

"Aw, how sweet," I said sarcastically.

"Seriously," he said, "how's school? Freshman year, right?"

"Very funny. I'm actually closer to being a sophomore. The school year's nearly over, remember?"

"Yes, well . . . I hear that you and our nosy neighbor are planning an extended sleepover. *That* should be interesting."

I had to laugh. Skip was so clever with words, and I honestly missed having him around. "If you promise to keep something quiet, I'll tell you a secret."

"You've gotta be kidding." He laughed. "This is definitely a first."

"Hush. If you keep it up, I won't tell you a thing."

"I'm all ears."

I took a deep breath. "Okay . . . here goes. I'm hoping to solve a mystery while I'm over at Old Hawk Eyes' place."

He was snorting now. "Let me guess. You're going to check out her high-powered telescope, right?"

"Count on me."

"My little sister, the super sleuth," he teased.

"I'm approaching adulthood, I'll have you know. In case you forgot, I'm going to be fourteen and a half in three days . . . April twenty-second."

"That's the most ridiculous thing I've ever heard. Nobody celebrates midyear birthdays."

"Well, *I* do."

"Figures."

I ignored his flippant response. We talked a few more

minutes, then he asked to speak to Mom. "I'll see you next Thursday afternoon," he said before hanging up.

"Remember, now—what you promised?" I reminded him of our secret.

"Won't breathe a word," he replied. "But I'll want a full report of your findings the minute I get home."

"Deal."

"Bye, little girl," he said.

If Mom hadn't suddenly come into the room, I probably would've chewed him out for yet another "little girl" comment. Enough was enough.

Still, I couldn't wait for Skip to come home. Especially now that he showed signs of wanting to be a true confidant, someone trustworthy to share in the results of my Spindler visit.

I handed the phone to Mom and headed back to my room and to my three remaining cats. Settling down on my bed, I thought of my brother's return home. Actually, I could hardly wait to see him again. Mainly because it seemed like such a long time since Christmas break—almost four months!

But Skip wasn't the only one coming home. Levi Zook—Rachel's brother—was, too. Truth was, I'd tried *not* to think of Levi's return. He liked me. Maybe too much.

In fact, the last time Levi had phoned, he kept using alliterated phrases—a word game I'd introduced to him. It kind of bugged me because it seemed everyone I knew was playing the Alliteration Game these days. The reason it bothered me, I guess, was that it started out to be a private thing between Jonathan Klein, the original Alliteration Wizard, and me.

Unfortunately, it was my own fault for involving my girl friends Chelsea, Lissa, and Ashley in the goofy game. But that was a whole different story.

Scooting off the bed, I went to my desk to think through my plan to locate my cat—the project I'd started before Dad knocked on my door. It would never do to sit around and wonder about Levi Zook anyway. He'd be here soon enough.

As for Jon Klein, he and I weren't exactly on the best terms lately, which was one-hundred-percent fine with me.

I picked up my pencil and made several attempts to create a lost-cat poster. But I was stuck, unable to write in alliteration-eze—the challenging language I used to be able to speak almost at will. But that was before thoughts of Levi Zook had crowded into my brain.

FIVE

"Abednego's missing," I told my girl friends after church the next day.

"Again?" Chelsea Davis asked, frowning. "Does he ever stay home?"

She *would* say that. After all, Abednego was known for disappearing off and on.

I sighed. "Actually, he got scared yesterday during that horrible storm."

"Oh, I remember," said Ashley Horton, our pastor's daughter, wide-eyed and obviously worried.

Lissa Vyner blinked her sad blue eyes at me. "Can we help?" she asked softly.

I nodded. "Maybe. I sorta thought of a plan."

"Like what?" asked Ashley.

"Well, it didn't turn out to be much, really," I said.

"C'mon, Mer, *tell* us. We're your closest friends," Chelsea insisted.

So I told them. I described how I'd sat at my desk last night till close to midnight, halfway waiting for Abednego

37

to wander home a drenched and frightened ball of fur, and halfway trying to make flyers that were clever and eye-catching to distribute around SummerHill.

"Your poster idea is positively terrific," Ashley said, her eyes smiling. Gushing was her trademark, and over time I'd learned to put up with it.

"So . . . tell us about your flyers," Chelsea said, twisting her auburn hair around her finger.

Lissa was silent, waiting with eyes fixed on me.

"Promise not to laugh," I said. "Honestly, I tried the alliteration thing, you know, for a catchy phrase or two, but I wasn't very successful. Abednego starts with *A*, and that's a hard letter to work with."

"No kidding," said Ashley.

"What about the Alliteration Wizard?" Chelsea inquired. "Have you talked to Jon?"

"Forget *him*," I spouted, glancing around to make sure Jon wasn't within earshot.

Chelsea's deep green eyes tunneled through me. "I can't believe you still feel that way. After everything you two have been through together."

I turned to go. "Not now, Chelsea."

❧   ❧

It was Lissa who followed me out the church doors and down the steps. The day was breezy and bright, with the promise of everlasting clear skies. A perfect day to walk home from church. And if I'd spotted my parents

38

right at that moment, I would've set out for SummerHill Lane on foot.

"Merry, please don't be upset," Lissa said, hurrying to keep up. "Chelsea didn't mean it. Not really."

I whirled around. "Of course she meant it! You were there—you heard what she said."

"No . . . no, I think you misunderstood" came the reply.

Shaking my head, I studied my wispy friend. Her wavy blond hair drifted softly around her shoulders, but it was the set of her lips that convinced me of her concern.

"Oh," I groaned. "This is truly horrible."

"It'll be okay," she said sympathetically. "You'll see."

But I felt dreadful. "Why do I have to get so freaked out over a boy?"

Lissa looked up from her long lashes. "Maybe it's because you still like him. Way down deep in your heart."

I couldn't bear it, especially from her. After all, last summer Lissa had fallen hard for Jon. And at the time, I'd considered him all mine. But now I wasn't one bit interested. At least, that's what I kept telling myself.

"Can we *not* talk about this here?" I snapped.

"Fine with me," she said softly.

I knew I'd offended her. "Look, why don't you come over this afternoon. We'll talk then."

"Okay, I'll call you after lunch," she said, turning to go.

Almost instantly, Ashley and Chelsea were on either

side of me. "We'll come help you make flyers," Chelsea volunteered.

"Okay with you?" Ashley asked.

I shrugged. "Sure, come on over."

"All right! Another alliteration affair," Chelsea announced.

I couldn't believe how good she was getting. "Wow, you've really caught on," I said.

"Amazingly well," Ashley said.

"So . . . watch out, Jon!" Chelsea said with thumbs up. "I'm ready to take you on."

Ashley grinned. "Hey, that rhymed."

"Shh! There he is," I whispered, pointing to a group of boys spilling into the courtyard.

Chelsea's face dropped. "I hope he didn't hear me."

"Let's not take any chances," I said.

"Meaning?" said Chelsea.

"I think we'd better split," I suggested, waving to the girls. "Call me about this afternoon."

They glanced over their shoulders at Jon, then grinned back at me.

Yee-ikes! I rushed to the parking lot. My parents were waiting in the car, windows down.

"Sorry," I muttered. "Got tied up talking."

"No problem," Dad said with a grin and started the car.

As he drove home, I leaned back against the seat, gazing at the cloudless sky and replaying the weird exchange between Chelsea and me.

After all these months, I still hadn't figured things out. Why did I have to get so giddy just talking about Jon Klein? Especially when I couldn't care less.

SIX

Not only did we make flyers, my girl friends and I, we tromped all over the SummerHill area that Sunday afternoon, searching the bushes and asking neighbors if they'd seen Abednego.

Chelsea came up with the coolest wording for our flyers. *Missing: a fussy, fat black feline—an amazing animal named Abednego*, it read. *Please contact Merry Hanson (owner), corner of Strawberry and SummerHill Lanes.*

The flyer was only partially alliterated but far better than anything I could've come up with. Probably because my brain wasn't functioning up to par. I was too caught up in the loss of my beloved pet. And, sadly, the chances of finding him seemed more dismal with every passing hour.

I'd even cried myself to sleep the night of Dad's retirement party, wishing the storm had never happened. Wishing something else, too—that Abednego wasn't such an exasperating pet, forever running off. Anguished, I'd stared hard at the long wall near my bed, unable in the dark to make out the minigallery of my own framed photography. Several pictures featured Shadrach, Meshach, and Abednego—my very first, and oldest, cats. Lily White had come into my life one year ago this month, so she was still the baby of the bunch.

"Where's your head, Merry?" called Ashley from across SummerHill Lane.

I snapped back to attention. "Uh, sorry, guess I was just daydreaming . . . about Abednego."

Unknowingly, I'd stopped at a quaint little spring house off the side of the road. It was the most serene place, almost like a playhouse made of old hand-hewn stone. Delicate willows draped their branches low, creating a leafy green fringed frame. The ideal setting for a country picture.

Ashley came running, followed by Chelsea and Lissa. "We have another idea," she said.

I was ready for a new approach . . . anything! We'd knocked on every neighbor's door in a one-mile radius. No one had seen Abednego. Not a single soul.

Ashley's hair was pulled back in a long ponytail, and her face shone with this most recent brainstorm. "Your neighbor is Old Hawk Eyes, right?"

"What about her?" I asked.

She paused, as if rethinking what she was about to say. Chelsea and Lissa hung on, waiting for Ashley's idea. "So . . . spill it out," Chelsea said.

Ashley took a dramatic deep breath. "Have you ever

come right out and asked Miss Spindler how she keeps track of everyone?"

"Well, no," I answered. "She's a very private person. Seems a bit nosy, if you know what I mean . . . but . . . why do you ask?"

We all looked at Ashley, waiting for her response.

Ashley raised one eyebrow in a questioning slant. "Well, I just thought the old lady might be able to find out where your cat is, that's all."

Chelsea chuckled. "Yeah, she seems to know the most intimate details about nearly everyone around here."

I nodded. "You can say that again."

"So what do you think?" Ashley said, eyes eager. "Why don't you ask her how she keeps tabs on things?"

I gave her a sideways glance. "Well, I've thought of doing that but never followed through."

"Why not?" asked Chelsea.

"Because it's like asking her to let me in on a big secret." I sighed, frustrated. "How *does* she spy on all of us?"

All three girls shrugged—nobody knew for sure. Bewildered, we began to walk back up SummerHill Lane. The sky was filling up with fluffy white cloud balls, reminding me of cats. Lots of beautiful alabaster cats.

Ashley got the Miss Spindler question rolling again. "You *did* ask her to keep an eye out for Abednego, right?"

"I sure did. In fact, Old Hawk Eyes' was the first place I went during the storm."

That seemed to satisfy her, and we set out for my

house. On the way, I glanced at my watch. "If we hurry, there might still be a few chocolate chip cookies left," I said. "My mom made a big batch yesterday after Dad's retirement party."

The prospect of homemade cookies made us pick up our pace, and we scurried past one Amish farm after another. Today was an off Sunday for the SummerHill Old Order church district, so lots of Plain folk were out visiting relatives and friends—the reason for so many buggies clattering up and down the road.

"Do you ever get tired of meeting up with the Amish?" asked Lissa.

"On the road, you mean?" I studied her, trying to figure out what she was really asking.

"Well, you know." She was clamming up on me.

"No, I don't," I replied. "Spell it out."

She shook her head, recoiling like she'd been hit.

"Look, Lissa. I can't read your mind. How can I know what you're thinking if you don't explain?" I asked gently. She'd suffered abuse at the hand of her father, and although he was taking therapy seriously and steadily improving, she still showed the emotional signs of a girl who'd been through the mill, so to speak.

She shook her head. "It's not important," she insisted.

"Yes, it *is* if you said it," Chelsea spoke up.

Ashley was nodding her head, encouraging Lissa to continue.

It looked as if we'd have to drag the question out of

her. Finally, after repeated pleas, she told us what she'd meant to say all along. "I'm curious about Levi Zook—his coming home for college break and all," she said.

I bristled at the comment. "If you're asking how I feel about him, I'm cool with our relationship," I confessed. "That's all I'm saying."

Chelsea ran her fingers through her hair. "But isn't Levi like in love with you or something?" As soon as she realized what she'd let slip, Chelsea covered her mouth, her eyes wide. "Oh . . . I'm sorry, Mer, I shouldn't have said anything."

I laughed it off. Had to. If I made too big a deal of it, she—*all* of them—would get the wrong idea. So I simply said, "Levi's a dear."

"And what about Jon? He's a dear, too, right?" Ashley piped up.

That got Lissa and Chelsea laughing. I joined in, hoping none of them would notice my cheeks growing warmer by the second. Truth was, I liked both boys, in spite of the pain Jon had put me through in the past. But as far as I was concerned, there was no rush to choose either one.

"Does Rachel Zook ever talk about Jon to you?" Chelsea asked, which surprised me to no end.

"Never," I said. "She's taking baptismal classes with her *beau*."

"Is a beau what I think it is?" asked Chelsea.

"Yep, and his name's Matthew Yoder. I wouldn't be surprised if she ends up marrying him."

The girls fell silent, and for the first time since we left the house, I heard birds singing.

"Rachel's pretty young to be thinking about settling down with a husband, but that's the way Amish do things. The younger you're married, the more children you'll be able to have," I explained.

"So . . . if you married Levi, would you have a whole houseful of kids, like the Amish?" Chelsea asked.

I felt my cheeks blushing. "Do we *have* to discuss this?"

"C'mon, Merry," Ashley spoke up. "Don't avoid the question. You know you're fond of Levi."

Fond? Where'd she ever get that idea? I wondered.

"Well, I can see this conversation is way out of hand," I told my friends. "Let's talk about someone else's romantic interests for a change."

Ashley's eyes darted away from my gaze, and Chelsea flung her long, thick hair to one side without saying a word. Lissa, on the other hand, just pursed her lips, trying not to smile.

Glancing down the road, I noticed Abe and Esther Zook pulling out of their dirt lane, the boxlike gray carriage filled with children. Rachel was along, too.

"Look, there's your future mode of transportation," Chelsea informed me with a stifled snicker. "If you marry an Amishman, that is."

It was high time to set them straight, once and for all. "Levi is no longer Amish," I said. "In fact, he's never taken the baptismal vow and joined his parents' church.

He's Mennonite now, studying to be a preacher at Bible school."

"Oh" was all Chelsea said.

"Case closed," I said, waving to the Zooks as their horse and buggy approached us.

Ashley ignored my comment. "What's Jon Klein want to be?"

"You mean when he grows up?" added Lissa.

I shook my head in playful disgust. "You three are every bit as mischievous as my wayward cat."

Chelsea clutched her throat. "Oh, tell me it isn't so!"

We burst into hilarious giggles and ran to my house.

SEVEN

At first I thought it was my lost cat jumping onto my bed, but then my bedroom burst to life with the early morning rays of the sun. Another too-real dream. One of many.

Mom called for me to "rise and shine" from her end of the hall. "Day's a-wasting," she added.

"I'm getting up!" Sliding out from under the light-weight blanket, I let my legs dangle off the side of the bed.

Shadrach, Meshach, and Lily White remained asleep, all three of them curled up tight against the dawn.

"Maybe today's the day Abednego comes home," I said, hoping it would be true.

Meow. Shadrach was all ears. And Meshach and Lily White leaped off the bed, stretched, and padded into the walk-in closet with me.

"You're truly lonely for Abednego, aren't you?" I whispered to my cat trio. "Well, I'm not giving up, so

51

don't you worry your furry heads, okay?"

Lily White rubbed against my bedroom slipper, and Meshach hung around like he hardly knew what to do with himself. Shadrach waited, intense eyes blinking only occasionally.

"Count on me to find him," I promised. But I had no idea what my next move would be. Abednego had already been gone for two days.

Meshach seemed terribly insecure and followed me to the bathroom door. "This is where I draw the line," I said, picking him up and kissing his soft, warm head. "I take showers *alone*."

Meow. It was as if he was pleading to be with me, and the sad expression on his face broke my heart anew. "We'll talk this afternoon when I get home from school," I told him.

I knew we wouldn't have much time to "talk"—Meshach and I—because as soon as the school bus dropped me off, I'd have to get myself packed and head over to Miss Spindler's.

In the shower, all I could think of was Abednego, possibly struck by lightning . . . or maybe only half alive.

❧ ❧

Downstairs, Mom had something akin to a royal feast prepared for breakfast. It was her typical Saturday morning brunch fare, except today was Monday. She'd gone to lots of trouble to cook up her favorite recipes because she and Dad were leaving for Costa Rica this afternoon.

"I want this to be a breakfast to remember," Mom declared as she served up little pancakes, cheese omelets with onions and green peppers, German sausage, and French toast with powdered sugar and maple syrup.

"You outdid yourself," I said, placing my napkin in my lap.

Dad raised his eyebrows. "Better be thankful, kiddo," he said. "I doubt Miss Spindler will come close to spoiling you like this."

I nodded, waiting for Mom to join us.

She dried her hands, then sat down, smiling across the table at me. "Ruby Spindler is an extraordinary cook, so I'm positive you won't go hungry."

Then I knew why Mom had chosen our eccentric neighbor to watch over me. She wanted someone to dote on me—look after me with meticulous care. "Oh, Mom, for pete's sake. Miss Spindler doesn't have to baby me." I was laughing.

"Well, she better give it her best shot," Dad said, winking at me.

I bowed my head for the prayer, grateful to have such thoughtful parents. Dad gave thanks for the meal in his soft, deep voice, and I knew I'd miss them. Even though they'd only be gone for six days.

🙢　🙢

Later, we hugged our good-byes. "Don't worry about me. I'll be just fine," I assured them. "And have a great trip."

Dad whispered in my ear, "Be kind to Old Hawk Eyes."

I giggled, trying not to distract Mom from her packing. Glancing at my watch, I grabbed my school bag and headed down the front stairs to the door. "My bus is coming," I called to them.

"Have a good day at school," Mom said from the top of the steps. "Remember to set the lamp timers before you leave for Miss Spindler's this afternoon."

"I'll remember."

"And take your cats along with you," Mom reminded.

"Naturally," I called up to her. Didn't she know I couldn't leave my precious babies alone in an empty house?

I headed out the front door and down the steps, thinking again of Abednego. My emotions were hanging by a thread—I missed him that much. And when I spied Chelsea on the bus, we talked of my runaway cat from the time I sat down until we scrambled to our lockers.

"We'll find him, Mer," she said, trying to soothe me.

"I truly hope so." I opened my locker and rummaged through the chaos in the bottom. "Because if I don't . . ." I paused.

"If you don't . . . *what?*" She leaned over and

gawked at me with those deep-set sea-green eyes of hers.

Tears welled up and began to spill down my cheeks. "Oh, great. I'm losing it at school," I bawled.

Chelsea draped her arm over my shoulder, and we huddled there near the bottom shelf of my locker. "It'll be okay," she kept saying over and over.

I wished my emotions hadn't run away with me because just then I heard a familiar male voice. Jonathan Klein's.

"Everything fine here?" he asked.

I gulped, wiping my eyes and taking a deep breath. Chelsea and I stood up together. "Hi, Jon," Chelsea said.

"You two look upset," he replied.

Chelsea nodded, glancing at me. "Have you ever lost something super significant?" she said, in alliteration-eze, no less.

Jon stepped back, blinking his brown eyes. "How significant are we talking?"

Chelsea waved him away. "Never mind, you wouldn't understand."

"Try me," he said, coming closer . . . looking at me.

I straightened up, stood tall. "What Chelsea's trying to say is . . ." I stopped, thinking how it would sound to blurt out that I was mourning my lost cat, wondering how Jon would react.

So far, he was smiling. "Mistress Merry, make me marvel."

I couldn't believe it. He wanted to play the word game—the Alliteration Game!

"What letter?" I mumbled.

"*C*'s," he replied, shifting his books from one arm to the other.

"Okay, here goes." I took a deep breath and began. "My crazy cat commands constant care," I said.

Chelsea jumped in. "Merry's cunning cat can't catch cold . . . he's old."

I turned around to face her. "Hey, that rhymed—and with alliteration, too!"

Jon was grinning. Not at Chelsea, at me! "So . . . let me get this straight," he said. "Your cat's both suffering and absent?"

"In plain English, yes," I said.

"So sorry . . . sad story," Jon alliterated and rhymed.

"Hey, what's with this?" I asked. "Is this the expanded version of the word game?"

Jon shrugged, his eyes still on me. "Could be."

Just when I thought I might fall in love with him, standing there sounding so charming, the bell rang for first period.

"Later, ladies," he said, heading down the hall.

Chelsea was giggling into my locker. "Didn't I tell you, Mer? This is so incredible!"

I grabbed my three-ring binder. "Keep it to yourself," I told her. "No one, and I mean *no one*, needs to know."

"C'mon! Jon likes you and you like—"

"Don't say it!" I interrupted and rushed off to home-room.

EIGHT

Right after school, Chelsea dragged me off to the bus stop, probably so I wouldn't end up with Jonathan. But since he rode the same bus we did, there wasn't any real way to avoid seeing him.

"What're you doing?" I whispered, pulling away from her at the curb.

"Trying to save you your share of heartache," she said.

"What's that supposed to mean?"

"You know." She motioned her head slightly toward the left of me.

"Jon?" I mouthed the word silently.

She nodded.

"Pretend we didn't see him," I whispered.

"Okay, quick! Open your English book."

But by that time, I could see Jon out of the corner of my eye. Still, I shuffled through my book, going along with her request.

No use. Jon came right up to us and stood next to me.

His sleeve actually touched my arm. "So what's with the expanded word-game notion?" he asked.

I smiled, not saying a word.

"I'll take you on," he said.

Chelsea started howling. "You're kidding! You aim to alliterate *and* rhyme . . . at the same time?"

I nearly choked. Chelsea was too good at this. A natural.

"What's the good word, Mistress Merry?" Jon asked, smiling down at me.

I shrugged, closing my English book. "It'll pose problems—take plenty of practice, probably." I watched the school bus head our way. "But then, so did alliteration-eze at first."

"Too true," said Chelsea, grinning at me.

The bus doors swooshed open, and we climbed on, one after the other, like three blind mice—three very smart ones.

It turned out that Jon sat in front of Chelsea and me, turning around to talk with us the whole way home. In no time, the three of us had decided the extended word game was a truly good challenge—the alliterated rhyme—but we hadn't decided what to call the game yet.

Strangely enough, I had a powerful feeling that Jon wanted this to be a special game—exclusive—between him and me. He never came right out and said it, of course, but it was the way he kept looking at me whenever we discussed it.

Chelsea, on the other hand, was having a great time

observing the two of us. I was afraid she was reading too much into things, though. And I let her know as we got off the bus at the willow grove, just down the hill from my house.

"Please don't get any ideas about Jon and me," I told her.

She was silent, her eyes twinkling.

"I'm not kidding, Chelsea!"

"What's not to get? I'm not totally dense. You're nuts for Jon—ditto for him."

I kicked a pebble, wishing for a different topic, anything but speculative talk on Jon Klein!

Chelsea kept babbling about how perfect he and I were together. I couldn't stand for her or anyone else declaring such things. That was my business and a very private matter, to say the least.

Finally we reached my house. Chelsea waved goodbye with a silly know-it-all grin, and I checked the mailbox. To tell the truth, I was glad for the solitude. Glad, too, that Chelsea hadn't asked to come in and help me pack. Miss Spindler would be waiting for me, and Meshach, my adorable Number Two cat, would be anxious for our "talk."

I thumbed through the stack of mail on the way up the walk. Hardly any bills or ads this time, but I noticed several pieces of personal mail. Two for Mom—one from Aunt Teri and the other from an old friend in the antiques business in Vermont. The third letter was from Levi Zook, addressed to me.

"Perfect timing," I muttered as I went around the house to the kitchen door.

My cats, all but Abednego, were waiting for me in the kitchen, near their bowl. Placing the unopened letter on the counter, I knelt down to stroke Shadrach, Meshach, and Lily White.

"Ready for a snack?" I asked, which usually brought gleeful smiles.

But today all they wanted was my tender touch. I fed them Kitty Kisses anyway, and they enjoyed the treat all the more because I sat on the kitchen floor with them.

"You guys are spoiled worse than rotten." I stroked Lily White, hoping she'd overlook my use of the male gender. "I love my prissy little lady, too," I said for her benefit.

While they ate, I stared at the envelope, high on the counter. Levi's letters had come fast and frequent right after his Christmas visit, but more recently they'd slowed down. *He's probably busy with his college work*, I thought.

I was busy, too. This last semester of school had been truly tough. Especially the amount of homework. Almost more than I could keep up with sometimes, even with Dad's voluntary assistance. Skip and everyone else had warned me that my freshman year would be a big transition. I just hadn't expected it to last clear into spring.

There was only one month of school left, and I could hardly wait for summer. But first things first. Tomorrow was my fourteenth-and-a-half birthday. Miss Spindler had no idea about it, but I was going to celebrate. Probably just me and my cats somewhere outside with my camera, a blue sky, and a sunny meadow filled with buttercups.

Then I thought of Abednego again. The pain of loss stabbed my heart. The worst of it was not knowing if he was dead or alive, sick or his robust self. *Where, oh where, can he be?* I wondered.

Meshach came over and nestled into my lap, taking up every inch of space. It was time for our talk.

"Your brother's out there somewhere," I assured him. "The Lord sees Abednego this very minute. I know He does." I sighed and continued. "If God can take care of an ordinary sparrow, He'll take care of our Abednego."

Meshach began licking his paws, and I knew my words, whether he understood or not, had calmed him.

Leaning back on my elbows, I stared at Levi's letter as Lily White rubbed against my arms. Shadrach curled up against my hip, nose to nose with Meshach. "Are we ready to stay with Auntie Hawk Eyes?"

At that, Lily White coughed hard and spit up a fur ball. I couldn't help myself; I started laughing. But soon my laughter rose to the next level, into a giggle. It almost sounded like Shadrach and Meshach were chortling a bit, too.

The phone rang in the middle of our hilarity. Gently, I lifted Meshach off my lap. "Sorry, little boy," I said, getting up. I reached for the wall phone.

"How's every little thing, dearie?" It was Miss Spindler.

"Things are fine," I said, touching Levi's letter. "I just got home from school and gave my cats a snack."

"Aw, the darlings," she cooed.

"Yes, they're pretty excited about coming to see you," I told her. I didn't say my cats were wildly anticipating the prospect of sampling *her* assortment of mice.

"Well, you come on over whenever you're ready, hear?"

I glanced at the wall clock. "Give me about an hour."

"That's right fine," she said.

I hung up the phone and picked up the letter, taking it to the privacy of my bedroom. Of course, there was no need, really. The house was void of humans.

Still, I sat on my bed, surrounding myself with plenty of huggable pillows. When I was completely settled, I opened the letter and began to read.

Dear Merry,

I hope you're enjoying the warm springtime weather there in SummerHill. Surely the farmers are busy plowing these days. Sometimes I miss farming and working with God's fertile soil. Now I'm tilling a different kind of soil and sowing the seeds of the Word. I've never been so happy, Merry. Coming here to Bible college was the best thing I ever set out to do.

The last time I phoned you, I said I'd be home for my Easter break, but just this week I've decided differently. Something's come up, and after much fervent prayer, I believe that my staying here is the Lord's will.

As for this summer, I will be taking more classes but

hope to get home for a quick visit with my family. Maybe around the Fourth of July. I'll look forward to seeing you then.

Meanwhile, please greet your mother and father for me.

Your friend,
Levi

I folded the letter, staring out the window. Levi was right about plowing season, all right. The days had been warm, accompanied by frequent afternoon showers. Perfect for enticing Amish farmers and their mules out at the crack of dawn. Hyacinths and daffodils were blooming everywhere, including those in my mom's flower beds.

Getting up, I went to my desk and opened the center drawer. *Your friend,* Levi had signed off this time.

I slid the letter into the drawer. Levi had found himself a new girlfriend. I was almost positive.

I suppose I should've reread his letter, double-checking my suspicions, but all I really needed to do was ask Rachel. She'd know, probably. At least, I guessed she would. But big brothers didn't *always* divulge their romantic game plans to younger sisters. Firsthand, I knew that to be true.

Sighing, I gathered up my school clothes for the next three days, as well as my pajamas, robe, and my camera equipment. Even though I tried not to let the news from Levi sadden me, I felt nearly hollow inside when I coupled the news with the loss of Abednego.

"When it rains it pours," I spouted into my closet. "Why'd he have to go and do this now?" But the more I thought about it, the more I realized I preferred the letter over having Levi call me, stuttering around, trying to explain why he wasn't coming home this week.

Still, it hurt. And I was honestly glad to be going to Miss Spindler's. Too bad her lookout room or telescope, or whatever, didn't stretch clear out to Virginia, to a Mennonite Bible college. And . . . to Levi Zook.

NINE

Miss Spindler was humming to her vegetable garden in the side yard as I hauled my suitcase up Strawberry Lane. Followed by my three devoted cats, I saw—on further observation—that she had every right to be truly captivated by her prim little rows of onions and radishes.

"Another green spring day in SummerHill," I said when she spotted me and my parade of pets.

"My, oh my, there you are." She smiled, eyeing the cats. "And those little furball critters of yours."

"We're all here, except Abednego," I said, hoping she wouldn't change her mind about the cats staying.

She shook her head pitifully. "The poor thing hasn't shown up?"

"Not yet," I said, glancing down at my cats. "But I haven't given up hope."

"We can only hope he's safe somewhere," she said. "Let's go inside and get you settled, dearie." She turned and marched up to the back stoop and opened the door. "We'll have some right good fun, I say."

I smiled, calling for the cats to follow.

Indoors, the kitchen smelled of delectable things, and I thought of Mom's wish for me to be well taken care of while she and Dad were out of the country. There were several pies laid out on a sideboard near the round dining room table.

Through the doorway, I could see the old-fashioned parlor, overflowing with quaint furniture from the past—fringed shades on tall floor lamps, a black steamer trunk doubling as a coffee table, and an old pump organ. Over-stuffed chairs and a large sofa were draped with white sheets, as if someone were remodeling. The formal living room had remained exactly the same since I first saw this house at age five, when my twin sister and I would visit for tea and apple pie with Mom.

"Well, come along now. I'll show you to your room, Merry."

I followed Miss Spindler up the steps to the second floor, keeping my eyes peeled for any clues to her spy tactics. *Anything.* Skip had asked for a full report, and I intended to give him the scoop. That is, if I could just steal away to the attic unattended.

"This is the guest room," said Miss Spindler, showing me into a spacious, wide room complete with a fireplace and two large dormer windows.

"What a pretty place," I said, spotting the lavender-and-blue Amish Spring Flower quilt pattern, probably made by Esther Zook and her relatives.

Miss Spindler's face was aglow with pleasure. I could

see she was thrilled to have me and my cats share her home, if only for a few days. "It's not many who come stay with me," she explained, frowning a bit. "Oh, I have my friends—a good many, too—but not much overnight company anymore."

"Thank you for having me," I said politely.

She showed me where there were extra hangers in the closet for my clothes. "There're empty drawers in the dresser, too," she said, sliding them out to show me, one after another.

"You've gone to too much trouble." I put my suitcase down.

"No . . . no, I always keep drawers empty, just a-waiting for folks. Don'tcha worry none about that." She smiled broadly, showing her teeth briefly—for a moment I thought she was going to hug me, too. But she came close and picked up my suitcase, carrying it over to the closet. She pulled out a foldable rack and placed my suitcase on top. "There you be, dearie."

Again I said, "Thanks," and began unpacking while she tiptoed away. I waited till her footsteps faded, then I slipped out of the room. Glancing around the hallway and second-floor landing, I wondered where the attic steps might be located. But I didn't feel comfortable heading off to do serious snooping just yet. I had to unpack first, then get the lay of the land, so to speak. Besides, my cats were antsy. I wouldn't risk having one of them interfere with my scheme to investigate Old Hawk Eyes' attic. Still, I was prickle-skinned with expectation.

❧   ❧

Miss Spindler's supper went far beyond delicious. Her Waldorf salad, homemade rolls, and chicken and dumplings were topped off with two kinds of pie—Dutch apple and cherry, with vanilla ice cream.

I chose the apple, and she warmed it up ever-so-slightly, just enough to make the ice cream scoop slide off the side.

When we were finished eating, Miss Spindler seemed altogether pleased with herself. "Well, looks like we ate for clear weather, didn't we," she said, clucking.

Carrying my dishes over to the sink, I offered to help. "Why don't you sit down and I'll clean up."

She waved her hand at me as though shooing a fly. "Aw, dearie, I'm sure you have something better to do— like homework or whatnot."

"I finished my homework in study hall."

"Well, what about that there retirement scrapbook your mama told me about? What about working on *that* tonight?" she said.

I'd brought along the developed pictures, all right, but I still wanted to do my fair share in the kitchen. And I told her so.

"Nonsense." Her blue-gray bob shimmered under the sink light. "While you're here, you're my guest." She flashed a ragged smile at me. "I want you to come again sometime, you know."

I nodded, feeling at a loss for words. The old woman

was bullheaded, that was for certain. She got something set in her mind and nobody but nobody was going to persuade her differently.

"If I can't help tonight, what about breakfast?" I offered. "You'd be surprised what a good cook I am—and even better at cleaning up!"

She nodded her petite head up and down as she stooped over the deep, two-sided sink. "Nothin' doing," she protested, and the finality of her words was clear. She was standing her ground. Old Hawk Eyes was like a thick-shelled Brazil nut—too tough to crack.

I wondered just how tough it would be to find her attic and see for myself what was going on up there.

❧   ❧

It turned out that I did work on Dad's scrapbook a little, and after about an hour of that, Miss Spindler and I played a rousing game of checkers. Not that she was so much better than I—she was just so shrewd and cautious of every move.

At last, it was bedtime. I knelt beside the bed and prayed for my parents and the building project in South Central America. I prayed for Levi, too, but only in passing. It was hard to focus in on someone I'd cared so much about, knowing his feelings were changing toward me, or already had.

Jon Klein showed up in my nighttime requests, but I only asked the Lord to help me not freak out so much in front of him. Nothing else.

My concerns for Abednego concluded my prayers. "Please, Lord," I whispered into the darkness, "keep my big, old cat safe. Send someone along to find him if he's hurt—to take care of him until *I* can again. Thank you for hearing my prayer. Amen."

TEN

The next day dawned sparkling bright, and morning birds warbled to their hearts' content. First thing, I thought of Abednego and prayed that today he might find his way back home.

I got up early on purpose so I'd have time to stop in and visit Rachel Zook before heading off to the bus stop. Miss Spindler didn't seem to understand why I wasn't all that hungry, so I told her where I was headed. I didn't tell her today was my midyear birthday, though. Most older folk don't understand that sort of thing. Guess they forget what it's like being a teenager. "Between twelve and twenty's a precarious spot," Dad had teased last September on my fourteenth birthday.

"I'll look after your cats for you," Miss Spindler called to me.

"Thanks, and keep an eye out for Abednego . . . just in case!" I hurried down over her sloping backyard, crisscrossing to my own, and stopped to check on the house. Searching under the gazebo first—and not finding him

73

there—I continued looking everywhere, in the back and side yards, and around the front porch. But Abednego was nowhere to be seen.

Inside, I dashed to my room, thinking if he'd returned through the kitty door in the garage, he might just be curled up on my bed. Fast asleep.

"Kitty, kitty, are you here?" I called, going from room to room upstairs.

In my parents' bedroom, I noticed the narrow door leading to the attic steps was ajar. Quickly, I closed it without thinking anything about it.

Not till later.

I was on my way to Rachel Zook's house, cutting through the willow grove, when it dawned on me where to look for Miss Spindler's attic steps. In her bedroom, of course.

But how would I get there without being caught?

Dismissing the discouraging thought, I ran across the open meadow, over the white wooden fence, through the pastureland, and down the side yard, to the barn. There I found Rachel cleaning up from the morning's milking.

She seemed surprised to see me. "Cousin Merry! What're *you* doin' over here so early?"

I had to laugh a little every time I heard her refer to me that way—as a cousin. But it was absolutely true, in a distant sort of way, at least. We had traced our roots back to common ancestors. Sure enough, we *were* cousins.

Looking around, I felt uneasy now that I was here.

What would Rachel think if I inquired of Levi this morning, clear out of the blue?

I went up close to her, glancing this way and that, making sure no one was around. "Have you heard from Levi?" I asked hesitantly.

"Jah, we had a letter from him yesterday," my friend replied.

"So he must've told you that he's staying in Virginia this week?" I had to phrase my question that way. Didn't want to come right out and state anything too presumptuous.

She kept her head turned, facing the cow. "S'pose he's too busy to bother with us during his school break," she said.

I didn't comment on her reply, and it was probably a good thing because in walked young Aaron with his father. Rachel surely must've sensed that I didn't want to discuss Levi with her father and younger brother in such close proximity, pitching hay to the mules a few yards away.

Thank goodness she didn't expect me to help sweep out the barn. I was already showered and dressed for school. There'd be no time to run back to Miss Spindler's and change before the bus lumbered down SummerHill Lane if I did happen to get my clothes dirty.

I checked my watch. Plenty of time left to chat with my Amish friend, but this just wasn't the right atmosphere for it. Not private enough. I tried not to gawk too curiously at Abe or Aaron, either one.

"What're you doing this afternoon?" I whispered to Rachel.

"Weedin' our Charity Garden, probably," she said. "Wanna help?"

I considered her invitation, but what I really wanted to do was go explore a meadow of yellow-faced daisies or maybe ride my bike over to the sun-dappled trees surrounding the spring house a mile or more down the road. "It's . . . well, sort of a special day for me," I said, dawdling.

She grinned back, and her blue eyes lit up. "Jah, I know."

"You do?"

"It's April twenty-second, right?" she said, wiping her hands on her long gray apron.

"Uh-huh."

"So then ya must be turnin' fourteen-and-a-half," she said, as if she'd known all along.

"That's right."

She gave me a quick hug. "We oughta do somethin' right nice, Cousin Merry. A wonderful-gut walk in the woods or whatever you say."

I had to smile. Rachel knew me almost as well as my own twin, Faithie, had.

"Are you sure you won't be missed in your garden?" I asked, not wanting to take her away from chores.

"Ach, I can weed after lunch. You just come on over after school's out. We'll have us a nice time together."

We walked outside into the sunlight. "Thanks for

being such a good friend, Rachel," I said, giving her another hug.

"Is Abednego back?" she asked suddenly.

I shook my head. "Not yet . . . but soon."

She frowned, her blue eyes more serious now. "Shall we go searching for your cat today?"

"My school friends and I spent Sunday afternoon combing the area. Nobody's seen him anywhere," I told her.

"He's probably out having himself a mouse-eating party," she said with a hopeful grin. "Jah, maybe we'll find Abednego today."

"That would be a good half-birthday present." I had to laugh because it was so true.

"Well, happy half birthday," she said, grinning at me.

"See you after a bit," I called, skipping down the Zooks' dirt lane to the road.

≥   ≥

My heart thumped *Jon Klein, Jon Klein* ninety miles an hour as I headed down the crowded school hallway. I couldn't figure out what was causing me to feel this way. Chelsea was absolutely right—saying that Jon and I had been through a lot together. Mostly rough times. He'd hurt me by flirting with both Chelsea and Ashley over the past eighteen months. And even Rachel Zook, last February, but that was two months ago already.

I sighed. Guess it was time to relinquish my grudge, if that's what it was. But I was worried. Could I really and truly trust the Alliteration Wizard?

"Merry, you're right on time," Jon said, waiting for me at my locker.

"What's up?" I asked, willing my heart to slow its pace.

"The game . . . the new one, remember?" His light brown hair was combed straight back on the sides, and today I spied gold flecks in his eyes. Funny, he was getting more handsome every time I saw him.

I remembered the game, all right. "I doubt I'll be able to hold my own," I said. "Creating alliterated phrases *and* rhyming ones all in the same breath, well . . . I don't know. Maybe Chelsea and you should try."

He was shaking his head slowly, eyes fixed on me. "I'm asking *you*, Merry."

It seemed strange not hearing his alliterated nickname for me—Mistress of Mirth or Mistress Merry. But there was something truly sweet about the way he'd said my name. *Merry*. Without fuss and frills.

The bell for homeroom rang before we could continue. In a way, I was glad. Mainly because I hadn't fully decided if I was up for the task. Alliteration-eze was one thing, but this rhyming idea . . . well, I just didn't know for sure.

I asked Chelsea about it in Algebra, and she was all smiles. "Let's go for it. I'm up for the challenge," she said, choosing the seat next to me.

"Maybe it's *your* thing," I said. "Yours and Jon's."

"Oh, Mer, how can you say that? You're the one who's

the *real* wit around here." She opened her notebook. "I'm just the tagalong."

I wanted to retaliate, debate her comment, but the teacher stood up and began discussing our homework assignment from yesterday.

Word Game Plus would have to wait.

If Jon hadn't seemed so interested in getting me involved, I might've blown the whole thing off. Let Chelsea and Jon have their fun. But I knew by the look in Jon's eyes, he wanted me to participate. He wasn't kidding. To tell the truth, though, I was more interested in digging up clues in Old Hawk Eyes' attic than dreaming up another word game.

ELEVEN

"Give me some sleuthing ideas," I said to Chelsea as we waited for the bus after school.

"What kind of sleuthing are we talking?" Her eyes were wide with intrigue.

I hadn't wanted to completely divulge my plan to snoop in Miss Spindler's attic. Skip's knowing was enough of a risk.

"Okay, Mer, level with me. What're you planning over at Old Hawk Eyes'?" asked Chelsea.

"Well . . ." I looked around to see if Jon or anyone else might be around to hear. "It's time someone found out the truth."

Her eyebrows jerked up. "The truth about what?"

"About . . . *you know*." I began to whisper. "How Ruby Spindler does it—spying on everyone."

She shrugged her shoulders and sighed. "Oh, that."

"Yes, *that!*"

Her eyes narrowed and she peeked at me with an inquisitive gaze. "I'd say you're extremely caught up in this."

"Too caught up? I'm a human being, for pete's sake!"

"A too-curious one, I'd say." Chelsea glanced over her shoulder. "I wonder what Jonathan would say about this idea of yours."

I pulled on her arm, yanking her back. "Don't tell him or anyone else, you hear?"

She started cackling. "Man, you sound as back-woodsy as Old Hawk Eyes herself. And Rachel Zook, too."

Something rose up in me. It was one thing to poke fun at my elderly, eccentric neighbor. It was quite another to belittle my Old Order Amish girl friend—one of the dearest and closest friends of my life.

"Rachel is who she is, and that has nothing to do with being backward or woodsy—neither one."

Chelsea stepped back slightly. "Well, aren't we the defensive one."

More than anything, I wished we weren't having this tiff. It was ridiculous, really. Besides that, months had passed since Chelsea had abandoned her declaration of atheism and started reading the Bible. And every single Lord's Day she attended Sunday school and church with me. What was going on between us at the moment was entirely unnecessary. Yet I had no idea why she was being so sarcastic.

"I didn't mean for us to fuss," I said softly.

The bus pulled to a stop, and we boarded without further comment. Chelsea slid onto our usual seat and stared out the window.

We rode along, not speaking for several miles. Then she turned to me and said, "I don't know what got into me, Merry. I'm not the least bit jealous of Rachel Zook. Honest, I'm not."

"And you don't have any reason to be," I replied.

She shook her head, then answered my original question. At last. "Seems to me you ought to be able to distract Miss Spindler somehow."

"Like how?"

"What do you want to investigate?" she asked me point-blank.

"Her attic."

"Good idea."

I smiled. "I think so, too."

"Maybe someone should give her a call, divert her attention, you know. Get her out of the house," Chelsea commented.

"I thought of that."

She stacked up her pile of books neatly. "But you simply can't get caught . . . that's the main thing."

"You're right. You want to give her a call sometime?" I asked, wondering what she'd say.

"Maybe." Chelsea had a faraway look in her eyes. "What I'd give to check out her attic with you."

"You're kidding? Really?"

She was nodding and grinning.

"Here's what I'll do," I said, thrilled we were seeing

eye to eye again. "I'll take pictures—lots of them, okay?"

"Great idea!" Chelsea was delighted.

"Aren't you glad I'm a world-class photographer?" I joked.

"Very glad . . . *silly*."

We stood up for our bus stop, and with a fleeting look out the window, I saw Rachel Zook weeding her mother's flower garden. All of a sudden, I could hardly wait to run away to a beautiful, private setting; I wanted to celebrate the midway point between fourteen and fifteen. With my Amish friend.

But first things first. I had an attic to attend to. And an old lady to visit with, as well.

Sure enough, Miss Spindler was waiting for me at her back door. "How's every little thing today?" she asked.

"School was fine."

"Easy, too?"

I had to think about that. "History and math weren't very easy," I admitted. "But most all my other subjects were." I didn't go on to say that socializing in the hall with a certain person wasn't all that easy, either.

"Any sign of Abednego?" I asked, hoping she had seen my funny feline.

"I thought you'd be asking about him," she said, a quizzical smile spreading over her wrinkled face. "So I done put my feelers out all over."

Feelers?

"What'd you do?" I asked, dying to see her telescope. The one she probably peered through, prying into the affairs of the world of SummerHill.

"Trust me, dearie. I'm doing my dead-level best to find that there kitty cat of yours." She clammed up after that, went right over and opened her fridge. I figured there was no point pushing the question.

Shadrach, Meshach, and Lily White were excited to see me, but not so eager that they didn't make a beeline to their milk dish after a few endearing comments and strokes.

On the table, a plate of peanut butter cookies and a tall, cold glass of milk awaited me. "You're gonna spoil me, Miss Spindler," I said, sitting down.

She smiled, making even more lines in her ancient face. "There, there, dearie," she said. "You've been studying your heart out all day at school, now, haven't you?" She didn't wait for me to answer. "You deserve a nice little treat, I daresay."

"Thank you," I said, remembering my manners as I chose a cookie from the offered plate. "Mm-m, they're still warm."

She nodded silently, her eyes glistening. I wondered just how lonely she was, living in this big house by herself.

"Ever think about getting a pet to keep you company?" I asked between mouth-watering bites.

"A pet? Well, my, oh my, I haven't ever thought of such a thing."

"The Zooks have some new kittens to give away," I mentioned.

She leaned her bony elbow on the table, looking into

my eyes. "Now, what on earth would an old lady like me do with a couple of frisky kittens?"

"Maybe you could start with one and see how you like it," I suggested, taking another cookie.

She sighed, gazing at my three cats having a snack of their own. "Well, I suppose it might be a good idea. Just don't rightly know where I'd put the dear thing."

"Cats like to wander the house," I told her. "They need plenty of roaming room. You have a two-story house . . . and an attic, too, right?"

She nodded, oblivious to my sneaky statement. "My attic's off limits to a cat, I'm afraid."

My ears perked right up. "Oh, why's that?"

Her eyebrows arched high over her eyes. "Well, now, a lady oughta have herself some privacy in a house this size, don'tcha guess?"

Surprised that she'd nearly come out and admitted to having a hideaway for meddling, I thought it best to drop the subject. Didn't want her to think I was prying, especially about something of great interest to me.

I thanked her for the after-school treat, then headed upstairs to change clothes for the afternoon.

"Tomorrow we'll have oatmeal and raisin cookies," she spoke up quickly.

"You don't have to bake a new batch just for me." I felt uneasy about her going out of her way for me. After all, she was no spring chicken.

"I'd be downright honored," she insisted.

So I left it at that.

On the way to my room, I took time to locate Miss Spindler's large bedroom. Stepping inside the doorway, I scanned the room briefly when I heard her rickety voice from below.

"Merry, dearie, I forgot to tell you that your parents phoned this morning after you left for school."

"They must be in Costa Rica . . . safe and sound?" I called, leaving her bedroom.

"They wanted you to know," she answered, her footsteps on the stairs.

Worried that I was about to be caught, I turned and fled to my room.

TWELVE

The meadow near the banks of Deer Creek was the perfect spot to spend the rest of the afternoon. That is, *after* we went scouring the bushes and underbrush for Abednego in the willow grove.

When we didn't find him there, we headed out to the highway, way at the east end of SummerHill Lane. He must have run far away to escape the lightning bolts and the crashing thunder.

"Maybe Abednego thought the noise and the lightning was coming from near the house," I told Rachel, wondering what might've been going through his furry head during the storm.

"Jah, maybe," Rachel said, out of breath.

We walked back toward her house, then cut across the north pasture to the meadow. There we sat in the tall grasses, encircled by golden buttercups and white and yellow daisies. We watched a pair of swallows flitter and dive after insects in flight.

"Has anyone ever seen Old Hawk Eyes' attic?" I

asked, shielding my eyes from the light of the sun.

Rachel played with the strings on her prayer cap and shook her head. "Nobody seems to know a thing about how she keeps up with all that gossip of hers."

"It's like she's connected somehow," I said, letting myself fall back in the grass. "She just knows so much . . . about all of us."

"Jah, plugged into the gossip line, I'd hafta say."

We talked about what it would be like for me to turn fifteen next fall and how it was for Rachel to be old enough to go to barn Singings on weekends.

"How's Matthew Yoder these days?" I asked, staring up at her silhouette blocking the sun.

She giggled and her cheeks turned crimson. "Ach, ya ain't s'posed to be askin' that sort of thing, Merry."

"So you *do* like him?"

"Matthew's the beau for me," she said softly. "We've been going to baptismal classes together. It's very important."

"Does this mean what I think it means?" I asked, anxious to know if she'd be joining the Amish church this year.

"I'm planning my future, jah. It's what's expected of me, I s'pose." She leaned back in the grass next to me, her cap askew.

"Then, you're not sure if it's the right thing . . . is that what you're saying?" It was nosy of me, but I had to ask.

"If I want to be Matthew's wife someday, I'll join the church. It's the only way to marry an Amish boy."

I turned to face her, the grass tickling my neck. "Are you saying he's already proposed?"

"Sorry, Cousin Merry, you know our traditions about going for steady. It's always kept a secret till two weeks before the weddin'."

I smiled. "Can't fool me. You're practically engaged, and you know it!"

With that, she got up and ran across the meadow. I chased her, laughing like a little child as ribbons of sunbeams floated all around us.

Later, after we'd worn ourselves out, we sat with our bare feet splashing in the creek. It was then that I asked her about Levi. "I have this feeling, you know."

"Far as I know, he ain't got a new girlfriend," Rachel said. "But, then again, I could be wrong. Things like that can happen so fast. Almost overnight, sometimes."

"I know, and that's okay . . . really it is."

She turned to me and reached to touch my hand. "It ain't okay, Cousin Merry, and you know it. Ach, not knowin' for sure is burning up your heart, and ya can't think of much else. Am I right?"

I didn't dare fess up. Not to Levi's sister, of all people.

She pulled her feet up out of the cool stream and dried them against the wild grass. "I was hopin' all along that someday you'd be my sister-in-law, ya know."

Any other time, I might've smiled at that. Pete's sake, I'd heard it enough times from her. But today I sat as still as the boulders along the creek bed, watching sunlight dance like teardrops on the water. "Someday's so far off when you're only fourteen," I whispered, still gazing at the little stars of light skipping and playing on the brook.

"You're fourteen and a half," she reminded me. "That's why we're here today . . . remember?" Picking up a pebble, she tossed it into the water.

"Caught between twelve and twenty," I muttered.

☙   ☙

Before going to bed, I decided to write Levi a note.

April 22
Dear Levi,

Thanks for writing again. You must be very busy at school, so I understand if you can't write as often as before. I've been busy, too.

I'm staying with Miss Spindler for a few days while my parents are in Costa Rica. Remember, they talked about going during MY Easter break? Anyway, it didn't work out, so they went this week, and I would've gone with them—to take pictures, like you suggested one time—but I couldn't miss that much school. So here I am.

Skip's coming home on Thursday afternoon to stay with me till Mom and Dad return on the weekend. My brother has a job near his college campus, so even though he's on Easter break this week, he's not getting much of a vacation from school, after all.

Today Rachel and I went looking for my ornery cat, Abednego. He's the one who's always running off. Well, I don't know for sure, but it seems he's not coming back this time, and I miss him. Only the Lord knows where he is now.

> *Maybe I'll see you this summer. Take care, and God bless you.*

Your friend,
Merry

I read what I'd just written and realized the note had a stiff sort of feel to it, and I wondered if Levi would notice. I hadn't meant to be standoffish toward him just because he wasn't coming home as promised. I was shielding myself, I guess. Didn't want to be hurt.

It wasn't long before Miss Spindler was calling me for supper. "Coming in a minute," I said, hoping to locate her attic stairs before heading down.

Once inside her bedroom, I opened two doors, both of which turned out to be closets. On the third try—bull's-eye!

I was absolutely baffled by what I saw. My eyes roamed up the steep, yet *carpeted*, beige steps. "Truly amazing," I whispered.

It looked to me as if Miss Spindler's attic had been finished, as in remodeled, and in as pretty a style as the rest of her house. Tomorrow, without fail, I would talk to Chelsea about setting up a time to phone Miss Spindler to occupy her time. I *had* to see this attic.

"Merry, dearie!" I was being paged.

Silently, I closed the attic door and hurried downstairs for supper.

Tomorrow!

THIRTEEN

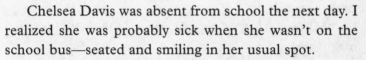

Chelsea Davis was absent from school the next day. I realized she was probably sick when she wasn't on the school bus—seated and smiling in her usual spot.

Later, when I asked Ashley and Lissa about her, Ashley said she'd called and asked for prayer last night. "She had a high fever, she said. Her parents were getting ready to take her to the emergency room," Ashley explained.

My heart sank. "Did your dad pray with her on the phone?"

Ashley nodded, sporting a grin. "Daddy was quite thrilled to pray for her. And something else."

"What?" I asked.

"Chelsea called Daddy her pastor."

"Really?" I was truly excited about that but concerned about Chelsea's physical problems.

"Has anyone called to check on her this morning?" I asked, glancing toward the pay phones near the school entrance.

Lissa looked at her watch. "I doubt that you have time to now."

I knew she was right. "Maybe during lunch."

The girls hurried off to their lockers just as I spied the Alliteration Wizard. Tall, lean, and relaxed, he strolled up to my locker. I honestly had to tell myself to cool it. He was just a guy, for pete's sake. Sure, he was an exceptionally good-looking one, but that was beside the point. There were oodles of cute boys at James Buchanan High. Still, why did my heart have to pound so hard when he came near?

"Mistress Merry," he said, greeting me with his usual nickname.

Funny, but I wished he'd revert back to calling me just plain Merry. Like yesterday.

We talked about Chelsea being sick and my cat being lost, mostly small talk. There was no mention made of his brain wave—the one about alliterating and rhyming in one breath. I was actually relieved. It was enough to wonder where Abednego had gone and contemplate my next move with Miss Spindler and her attic—especially now that Chelsea wouldn't be able to distract her with a phone call—let alone ponder if I was up to the task of expanding my cerebellum by adding yet another facet to Jon Klein's word game.

"I wonder . . . could you do me a favor?" I blurted.

His gaze and smile made me almost forget what I was about to say. "Whatever you wish," he said.

"You've met Miss Spindler, right?"

He frowned, thinking. "Not really . . . not formally, at least."

I wondered if this was such a good idea, after all.

"What's the favor?" he prodded.

"Could you give her a call after school today?"

"Old Hawk Eyes?" He chuckled, reaching up and smoothing his hair back with one hand. "You want me to call an old woman I don't remember ever meeting?"

"Would you, *please*?"

"Only if you give me some ideas—you know, what I should say to her," he insisted.

I sighed. "Well, let's see. You could talk about her vegetable garden or . . . her need for a pet. That's it! Tell her you know of someone—that would be Rachel Zook—who has way too many cats. I've already put a bug in her ear about that. What do you think? Nice topics for conversation, right?"

He offered a slight smile. "I think you better tell me what this is about, Merry, because I have a feeling you're up to something. Something super strange."

Jon was absolutely right. So I told him what I planned to do while he kept Miss Spindler on the phone.

He shook his head, laughing. "You're going to be upstairs in her attic?"

"Uh-huh."

"Doing what?"

"Just spying a little."

He seemed interested. "Checking out her attic for what?"

The bell rang just then, and we had to conclude our talk.

"I'll fill you in at lunch," I promised.

He was still in a daze. I saw confusion in his eyes.

Then it hit me.

Oh great, I thought, *this is the dumbest thing I've ever done!*

❧ ❧

It turned out that something must've come up for Jon over lunch hour, because he never showed up. I told Ashley and Lissa about my quick chat with Chelsea's mom before lunch. "Chelsea was going to distract Old Hawk Eyes—with a phone call—but she's too sick to do it. Really sick."

They listened, wide-eyed, as I filled them in. "Chelsea's got scarlet fever and won't be back to school for over a week."

"Scarlet fever?" Lissa gasped. "Don't people die from that?"

I tried to calm her down, explaining that back in the "olden days" people didn't have strong antibiotics to kill the virus.

"Hey, wait a minute," Ashley said, clutching her throat. "It's contagious . . . and weren't we exposed to her last Sunday afternoon?"

"You're right. All of us went looking for Abednego together," I said, thinking back to whether Chelsea had complained of a sore throat or anything else. "The best thing to do if you've never had scarlet fever is get plenty of rest and drink lots of water," I told them what Chelsea's mom had just advised me over the phone. "And take extra vitamin C—that might help you, too."

My comments seemed to satisfy Ashley's concern. Lissa, however, was still frowning. "Someone will have to take Chelsea's homework to her, right?"

I shrugged it off. "I'll take it. I'm not afraid."

"You sure that's a good idea?" Ashley asked.

"I'll be fine. Don't worry." I meant it. "When I was little I had a mild case of scarlet fever."

"You remember?" Lissa asked.

"Barely, but yeah."

"Well, then, you're the girl for the job," Ashley said.

"Say that with all *j*'s," I dared her. But she didn't even try.

I excused myself and got up from the table. "Have to find where Jon's hiding out. He and I have something to settle." I didn't want to say more.

Lissa's eyes blinked ninety miles an hour. "Uh, really? Is this something *we* oughta know about?"

I brushed off her comment. Didn't need to let her in on my wild scheme. Maybe later, but not now.

"Are you and Jon getting . . . you know, back together?" Lissa asked out of the blue.

I almost choked. "We were never 'together' in the first place." *Except in my heart*, I thought.

"But you and he—"

"Nope, we were always just friends." I paused, remembering the days when he and I were strictly alliteration buddies. Back before anyone else knew about the word game. "Just good friends," I repeated.

"So then, what's the big secret?" Ashley came right out and asked.

I debated whether to divulge my plan. Students all around us were eating and chattering, some laughing and making jokes at their tables, others cramming for tests—spreading homework out in front of them.

"Merry?" said Lissa. "We think it has something to do with Miss Spindler."

I couldn't hold it in another second. "You're right. It's about Old Hawk Eyes . . . and her attic."

"How does Jon fit in?" Ashley asked, reaching for her soda.

"Very carefully" was all I would say.

"Aw, tell us," Ashley persisted.

"Gotta run," I said, leaving the table, their pleadings ringing in my ears.

FOURTEEN

After school, I took Chelsea's homework assignment to her house and gave it to her mother at the door. It was good to see Mrs. Davis looking so fit and perky, her cheeks rosy and eyes bright again. She'd been through quite an ordeal last fall, and I knew God had answered many prayers.

"Thank you, Merry," she said. "I'll be sure to tell Chelsea you dropped by."

"Give her this, too." I held out a get-well card I'd made during study hall. "It's from Ashley, Lissa, and me."

"How sweet of you. You're very kind."

I waved and headed down the front steps to the road. Running down SummerHill Lane was easy from Chelsea's house to mine. It was the steep slope that turned left at Strawberry Lane that took the wind out of me.

At precisely 4:15 the phone rang at Miss Spindler's. I

held my breath, leaning over the banister upstairs, listening.

"This is Ruby Spindler," I heard her answer the telephone. Then, for the longest time, there was silence on her end.

Johnny-on-the-spot, I dashed to her bedroom and checked the caller ID on the bedside phone table. Sure enough, Jon Klein had come through for me, just as we'd secretly concocted at my locker after school.

Cupping my hand over my mouth, I held in the giggle that threatened to spill out. Quickly and quietly, I approached the door that led to the attic, thinking that I'd love to know what Jon was saying right now! Was he showing off his alliteration-eze for her?

Once I was on the other side of the door with my foot on the first step, I turned and closed the door behind me. Silent as springtime.

Then, taking the stairs two at a time, I sprang up into the attic, once again surprised at the wood-paneled walls, finished ceiling, and flecked beige carpet.

What I saw at the top of the steps, I'd never have believed in a million years if I wasn't seeing it with my own eyes. This was an old lady's attic, for pete's sake!

I looked around, amazed. Here was a room high in the eaves, completely set up as an office, with built-in oak cupboards and a wide computer desk.

"A computer? What's Old Hawk Eyes doing with a computer?" I muttered.

Truly incredible.

I crept closer to the unusual sight before me. Surely, this was an outlandish dream, nothing more. But my eyes told a different story. This was *not* a dream. My fingers were touching the desk, the top of the computer, and the small desk lamp, declaring the reality of the whole setup.

Miss Ruby Spindler must've had a professional come in and install the computer for her. It was the weirdest thing. Why on earth did an old woman need all this high-tech equipment?

Wait'll Rachel hears about this, I thought. *And Levi!*

Yes, Levi Zook would get a big charge out of this. So would Jon Klein and all my girl friends at school. In fact, they'd have a hard time believing this place really and truly existed.

That's when I remembered my camera. I'd forgotten to bring it along. *What were you thinking?* I reprimanded myself.

Turning to go down the steps to retrieve it, I heard my name being called. I froze in place, looking every which way—wondering where I might hide.

"Merry, dearie," Miss Spindler called from what sounded like her own bedroom. Just below the attic room!

Yee-ikes! I had no idea what to think or do.

"Merry? Can you hear me?" she said again.

My heart was pounding in my ears so hard, I couldn't begin to think of a solution to my plight. The old lady wanted a reply, and if she didn't get one soon, she might come looking in the attic. I couldn't have that. There had to be another way!

Glancing around the long, narrow room, I noticed a small closet door smack-dab in the center. An odd place for a door, to be sure.

Without a second thought, I darted inside. I was surprised to see the door led to more steps, straight to the roof of the house and to a hinged double-swing door. The latch was unlocked, so I pushed hard and it opened easily.

Standing up, I saw that the roof was actually a widow's walk perched on top of the main roof of the house. I paced off the flat, square area, flabbergasted at this incredible lookout. Taking in the sweet springtime air, I stopped to lean on the wooden railing that surrounded the observation platform, letting my eyes roam the expanse of sky and landscape below. "Of course," I said to the air and trees, "this is how Old Hawk Eyes sees so much!" But honestly, I'd never noticed the widow's walk from our house. Probably because the enormous trees blocked it from view.

I saw clearly the road that ran in front of my parents' home and all the way down past the Zooks' private lane. I saw the white gazebo in my own backyard, where strangers had slipped a baby in a basket and left her there, and the willow grove where my abused friend had waited for me in that moonlit November night so long ago.

Sighing, I knew, sure as anything, how the nosy old

lady had spotted little Susie Zook being harassed by tourists last summer. How she'd seen me riding with Levi in his courting buggy, too.

Beneath me, there were noises coming from the attic, and I assumed Miss Spindler was still searching for me. But I remained silent, not wanting her to know that I'd discovered her secret. At least, part of it.

"Merry, are you up there?" she called.

She was on her way up! I was going to be caught whether I liked it or not.

I wondered, *What should I do?* and glanced over the side of the railing, determining if I could jump to the lower roof level. Carefully surveying the distance, I decided not to risk a broken leg or two. I wasn't *that* stupid.

"Merry?" There she was again. Miss Spindler was coming. I was burnt toast!

There was no other choice but to answer. And I was opening my mouth to call to her when I heard a chiming sound, like beautiful orchestral bells.

Whatever the sound was, it silenced Miss Spindler. She actually stopped calling! Not sure whether to shout for joy or hold my breath, I sat on the railing and looked out over the valley below. Rachel Zook was coming in from the barn, followed by Aaron and her younger sisters. They were finished with afternoon milking, most likely.

To the south of me, I scanned the soon-to-be acres and acres of cornfield across SummerHill Lane from the front of my house. To the west, I enjoyed the leafy tops of maple, spruce, and elm trees. I could not see as far up the hill as Chelsea Davis's house, though. It was situated on the crest of the hill, higher than even the roof of Miss Spindler's house. Back to the north, I could see the sun-dappled meadow where Rachel and I had spent our afternoon together yesterday.

I'm queen of the mountain, I thought. Checking my watch, I suddenly realized I'd not heard a sound from Miss Spindler for quite some time.

Now might be as good a time as any to head back into the attic. Maybe, just maybe, I could sneak back down to my room and she'd never have to know where I'd been.

On tiptoes, I inched my way back into the attic, peeking through the crack in the door before heading inside.

The place was deserted.

Whew! I was home free!

Just as I crept past the computer desk, though, the chimes I'd heard before *dinged* again. I glanced toward the screen.

Wonder of wonders! Miss Spindler, it said, had an email message. I stepped closer for a better look. No, it said she had *five* new emails! Truly amazing. Old Hawk Eyes was as thoroughly modern as any person I knew.

Not wanting to pry, I noticed a note pad lying near the mousepad on the desk. To my surprise, I saw a long list of names. *Email pals,* it read—and at the top were printed the words: *Windows on the Hill.*

"What's going on?" I whispered, investigating further—snooping around the desk area but not reading her email messages. "Wait'll Skip hears about this!"

Miss Spindler was truly plugged in and turned on. She was in touch with the world in a way I'd never dreamed possible. *Never!*

But what could "Windows on the Hill" mean?

I had to find out!

FIFTEEN

Stepping inside Miss Spindler's attic and seeing her computer setup, email and all, was one thing. Trying to decipher what was actually going on up there was something else altogether.

It turned out I had no time to find out for sure. The supper bell was ringing downstairs mighty powerfully. I had to scoot. And fast.

After supper dishes were cleared away, Miss Spindler asked if I'd had a nice after-school nap.

"A nap?"

"Why, yes, dearie, I called and called to you. I just figured you were fast asleep . . . poor thing, tired from all that there book learnin'." Her eyes were smiling, as if she knew I hadn't been sleeping at all. To tell the truth, it seemed as if she was playing a little game with me.

"I wasn't napping," I said.

"Oh?" She tilted her head to one side. "Well, I was mistaken, then, I do suppose."

"Yes" was all I said, but I was dying to ask her about

Jon Klein's phone call. Since I wasn't supposed to know anything about it, I'd have to wait till she brought it up on her own. *If* she did.

So I tried to be patient all through a game of Scrabble. She simply rearranged her wooden tiles, one after the other, taking her sweet time, not talking about Jon's phone call. All the while, I stewed. What *had* he said to her during that time? *Maybe he taught her how to speak alliteration-eze*, I thought comically and almost laughed while Miss Spindler racked up a triple-word score.

"Well, now, dearie, let's see if you can top that." She'd said it with a spirit of determination—and victory.

Now what was I to do?

Shuffling my tiles, frustrated at the appearance of a *q* without an accompanying *u*, I planned my pathetic move.

"What's the matter tonight, Merry?" she asked, sticking a pencil into her blue-gray puff of hair.

I glanced at the clock. "I better get to my homework."

She was shaking her head. "Nothin' doing, dearie. Not before you take your turn. Then we'll tally up the score."

There was no way out. I had to follow her wishes. After all, I was the guest here. Still, I *had* to know about that elaborate computer setup of hers. And her conversation with Jon.

I took my turn and counted up a measly eight points. Before I left for my room, Miss Spindler added up the score. She was the winner. "Thank you, Merry, for being such a right good sport," she said as I pulled out my chair.

"But I'm wondering if there might be something else on your mind, dearie?"

I wasn't rude, but I dodged the question. "One of my school friends is waiting for me to call," I said. "Do you mind?"

"No, no, I'll put the game away. You run along."

Deciding it would be best to call Jon from the upstairs hall phone, I darted up the stairs and dialed. Thank goodness, he answered on the first ring. "You'll never guess what I found in Miss Spindler's attic," I said, not even saying who I was.

Jon was all ears. "I'm listening, Merry."

"On second thought, I'd better wait to tell you at school," I said, thinking I shouldn't reveal anything over the phone. "But it's big . . . I mean *big*."

"Okay, I'll meet you at your locker, first thing."

"That's nothing new," I said, chuckling.

"Oh really? Well, if that's the case, let's not stop now." His laugh was warm and encouraging.

I was anxious to hear about his phone call. "What did you and Miss Spindler talk about this afternoon?"

He paused. "Maybe I should make *you* wait till tomorrow, too."

"Aw, don't be a spoilsport," I said. "It's not such a secret, is it?"

"Might be, Mistress Merry." It was his cue for me to play the word game.

"*M*'s?" I asked.

"Maybe," he said.

I stopped to think. "Might Merry make many more mindless mistakes?"

"Wow—great stuff."

"That's not *m*'s," I insisted. "Start again."

"Nope, I give up. You win today. You win for always."

"What?" This was truly amazing.

"You heard me, Merry. You're the Alliteration Queen. I pronounce you the victor."

"You're kidding, right?" After all these months, he was naming *me* winner?

His voice grew soft just then. "I'm tired of it."

"Alliteration-eze?"

"That and Chelsea's idea to add rhymes to everything." He stopped, and I could hear his breathing. "You know what I'd really like, Merry?"

I was breathless—could hardly speak.

He didn't wait for me to answer, and I was glad. "I want to start talking to you normally. It's too hard to make real sense of things when you're all tongue-tied over *t*'s . . . or, well, you know."

I knew exactly what he meant. But I wasn't feeling so articulate at the moment. I had a funny feeling he was trying to tell me something very important.

"Merry . . . you still there?"

"I'm here," I said softly.

"Good. I'll see you tomorrow."

"At my locker, right?"

"No . . . better yet, I'll save you a seat on the bus."

My tongue felt permanently tied, for sure. All I could

do was mumble something totally unintelligible when he said good-bye.

Hanging up the phone, I honestly felt a bit dizzy. I'd been waiting nearly forever for this moment, and I could hardly make it down the hall to the bedroom.

My cats were sympathetic enough. We snuggled, the four of us, on top of the old feather bed. "Somebody likes me," I told them softly. *Very* softly.

Leaning back against the fat, over-plump pillows, I daydreamed of walking down the halls of James Buchanan High with Jonathan Klein at my side.

"There's only one other thing that would make me as happy as this," I said to Shadrach, Meshach, and Lily White. "Finding Abednego would be truly great."

They seemed to understand—at least the brothers agreed with my remark. I wasn't so sure about Lily White. She seemed entirely satisfied, sharing the attention with one less cat.

"Tomorrow I'm going to search for him again," I told them. "Cats as big and black as Abednego don't just vanish from the face of the earth."

His brothers must've understood because both of them hopped off the bed and leaped up to adjacent, wide windowsills and peered out into the darkness.

"We go home tomorrow afternoon," I told Lily White. "You'll get to see big brother Skip again. Won't that be nice?" I cuddled her close to my face, and her purring was strong and steady.

"Miss Spindler's got herself a computer . . . and

email, too," I whispered against the soft, furry head. "Isn't that the tallest tale you ever heard?"

When I said the word "tale," Lily White flapped her delicate white one against my arm. "Okay, kitty-girl, down you go."

It was then I remembered something Old Hawk Eyes had said. *"I done put my feelers out all over."* Had she emailed lost-cat messages to her computer pals? Is that what "putting feelers out" meant?

"I'm gonna find out, for sure," I said, opening my math book. "First thing tomorrow."

SIXTEEN

Jon's broad smile lit up the entire school bus. I tried not to show my giddiness, and he was polite and slid over next to the window as I sat down.

Fortunately, Chelsea was nowhere in sight. Had she been on the bus, saving a seat as she always did, I would've had some big explaining to do.

"Who goes first?" Jon said.

I couldn't help but smile. He was more than eager to hear of Miss Spindler's attic hideaway. "I've got the most incredible news for you." And I told him about the old lady's computer setup, complete with email capability.

"Wow, that *is* news," he said.

"What I wonder is how she's kept it a secret."

Jon nodded. "Who knows how long she's been using her email to keep tabs on people."

I gasped. "So that's it! She must be sending mail to the SummerHill neighbors up and down the road, getting the scoop on everyone that way."

Grinning, Jon leaned against the window, turning to

face me. "She told me about some of those neighbors yesterday on the phone. You'll be surprised when you hear who they are."

"Really? Like who?"

"For starters, Matthew Yoder's dad owns a computer."

"You're kidding—Rachel's boyfriend's dad?"

"He can't have it in the house because the Amish bishop won't allow it. But Mr. Yoder has permission to use the computer for his carpentry business."

I was shocked. "But they're Old Order Amish, for pete's sake!"

"I was surprised, too. But Miss Spindler says she and Matthew's mother exchange email almost every day, along with a lot of other Plain folk, including Ben Fisher's mom, way down at the end of SummerHill Lane." His eyes were on me as he shared this amazing tidbit of information.

"This is so crazy," I said, leaning on my book bag. "How'd you get her to tell you this?"

He glanced down at his books for a moment. "I guess she just wanted to talk. She's a lonely old lady, you know."

I shook my head at him. "I think you'd better level with me, Jonathan Klein! What did you *really* say to her?"

"Let's just say I charmed Old Hawk Eyes."

Charmed? I laughed out loud.

"I'll bet you did." I stared at him, knowing full well he wouldn't divulge his tactics. At least not without some prompting. "So . . . did you charm her with alliteration?"

"Only for a while, but soon she was intrigued with the word game, so she decided to try it herself."

I laughed. "Miss Spindler and you?"

"Hey, everyone else is speaking it. Why not?" His eyes were twinkling mischief. "The old lady knew all along where you were, Merry," he said. "She figured you were checking out her attic yesterday when I called."

"What?"

"Miss Spindler went along with it . . . guess she didn't want to spoil your fun."

One wacky revelation after another! "So does she want me to ask her about what I saw in the attic?"

"Not only is she restless to tell you, she's hoping you'll help her sift through all her email messages," he replied.

"Why me?"

"For some reason, she seems to think she can trust you, Merry." He paused, looking right at me. "And something else."

"There's more?"

"She has trouble seeing her computer with her tri-focals—makes her neck stiff, she said. So maybe she'll ask you to help her out sometime."

"Why's she getting so much email, do you think?" I asked.

"She's enjoying all her new friends, I guess."

The bus pulled into the school parking lot and stopped at the appointed curb. My most miraculous moment was about to end. I wanted it to last forever, sitting here beside the cutest boy in the whole school. No, the whole county.

Suddenly, I realized I hadn't taken Levi Zook into consideration. Guess I thought of him less as a boy and more as a young man. Maybe . . .

"See you at your locker?" Jon asked. His smile was as blissful as it was big.

"Okay." And we walked into the school together.

Later, when the bell rang, my yesterday's daydream came true. The former Alliteration Wizard and the reigning Alliteration Queen walked side by side down the swarming, yet seemingly silent, hallway.

❧   ❧

After school, my cats helped me pack. Well, they didn't actually do anything except curl up in the wide and golden sunbeams that spilled into the guest room from each of the dormer windows.

"We're going home," I sang, trying not to think about Abednego. Here it was Thursday, nearly a week since the storm had scared him away. I missed him terribly, ornery and spiteful as he was.

Looking in all the empty drawers, on the closet floor, and under the bed, I made sure nothing was left behind. Then I realized what a wonderful, old-fashioned bedroom this really was. For a fleeting moment, I actually thought I might miss this quaint place.

"Come on, little ones," I said to my snoozing, perfectly contented cats. "We have to tell Miss Spindler good-bye."

Surprisingly, they got up, stretched, and followed me downstairs, where Miss Spindler was waiting, all smiles.

"I hope you had a right nice time, dearie," she said, filling my backpack with a plastic container of homemade cookies.

"Oh yes, I did." I glanced down at my cats. "I should say *we* did. Thanks again. I know it took a lot of worry off my parents' minds while they're gone." I paused. Now was a good time to apologize for sneaking around in the old woman's house. "I shouldn't have gone snooping in your attic, Miss Spindler. My parents would die if they knew about it. I'm sorry," I said, meaning every word.

"Forget it, dearie," she said and patted the box of cookies through the backpack. "Remember, now, there's more where these came from . . . and you and your brother are gonna be all alone over there. If you need anything at all, just give me a holler. Dessert, ice cream . . . you name it. I'll even bake you up some pie."

I was chuckling. "And the same goes for you, Miss Spindler. If ever you need anything, just let me know."

That's when her eyes got big and round, like coat buttons. "Come to think of it, Merry, dear, there *is* something I could use some help with." Then she waved her hand, shooing me off for home. "Aw, shucks, it'll wait till you get yourself settled in again. Tell that big brother of yours hello from this here neighbor, ya hear?"

"I will," I promised, eager to find out if what she

needed help with was her email messages. I don't know why it intrigued me—her pushing eighty and doing the high-tech thing. But then again, this was the same old lady who drove a hot red sports car all over SummerHill.

SEVENTEEN

My brother was more excited to hear about the attic "find" than he was glad to see me, I think. He got all caught up in my story right off.

"Won't Mom and Dad freak?" Skip said, face aglow. "I mean, this has gotta be the biggest story in all of Lancaster County. Except maybe that drug bust among the Amish out east of town."

"Hey, I wonder if we should call up the newspaper?"

Skip sat at the kitchen table. "The media would be more than happy to sensationalize a story like this." He helped himself to some of Miss Spindler's cookies. "I can see the headlines now: 'Plain Folk Chat With Hot-Rodding Spinster on Net.' "

Laughing, I poured him a tall glass of milk. "I think we better keep the media out of it and just enjoy the wackiness ourselves."

He pulled out a kitchen chair for me, and I was surprised at his gentlemanly gesture. "Who else knows about this?" he asked, breaking the stillness.

"Only Jon." I thought about it. "And some of my girl friends."

"They knew about you investigating Old Hawk Eyes' attic?"

I nodded. "But they haven't heard what I found. Least, not my girl friends."

Skip drank half the glass of milk straight down. "Are you still doing that weird word thing with Jon?" he asked.

"How'd *you* know about that?"

Leaning back on the chair, he devoured another cookie. "Jon's sister talks about it every now and then."

"Oh, so you and Jon's sister are still writing love letters?" I teased.

He couldn't contain the pink color that crept into his face. "That's none of your business," he said flatly.

"Well, it's gonna be my business if Nikki's my sister-in-law someday!"

He sneered—his old self was showing through. "And if I marry her and you marry Jon, our kids will be brousins—closer than cousins—get it?"

I shook my head at him. This was a pitiful conversation. "I'm going upstairs," I said, getting up from the table.

"Who's cooking tonight?" he asked, looking worried.

"You are." With that, I disappeared up the kitchen flight of steps and headed to my room. I made myself comfortable on the bed and spread out the scrapbook of my dad's retirement party. Time to finish my scrapbook project. I wanted Dad *and* Mom to be surprised when they arrived home this Saturday.

The phone rang an hour later, but I ignored it, letting Skip get it for a change. When he didn't call for me right away, I figured it must be for him. *Probably Nikki Klein*, I thought. She had always been one to chase after my brother.

"Merry, it's for you," Skip hollered up to me.

"I'll be right there!" Scurrying down the hall to Mom and Dad's bedroom, I picked up the phone. "Hello?" I said, out of breath.

"Merry, dear, it's Miss Spindler."

"Oh, hi. Is everything all right over there?"

She snickered. "That's *my* line, dearie." *How's every little thing* was what she always said—first off.

"Yes . . . well, I forgot. Sorry."

"Oh my, there's no need to apologize," she said. "I just thought I'd call and check with you about supper plans."

Supper plans?

Then I remembered my brother was in charge of the kitchen. At least, I'd told him he was cooking tonight. "Uh . . . yes, we're open to suggestions," I said rather quickly.

"That's just what I hoped to hear," said Miss Spindler. "I made a ravioli casserole that's just downright too big—family size, I daresay—and, well, since there ain't much of a family over here, I thought I'd invite myself to supper."

I looked up to see Skip standing comically in the doorway, motioning for me to say yes. Which I was more than happy to do.

"Aren't you the lucky one," I told Skip as I hung up the phone. "Somebody who can actually cook is bringing pasta for supper."

"Hallelujah!" he sang.

I was mighty glad about it, too. But I couldn't help wondering what Miss Spindler had on her mind. Surely there was something.

Quickly, I dialed Ashley Horton. I filled her in on everything she'd missed since my snooping expedition in the refurbished attic across the yard from me.

"I'm not one bit surprised," Ashley said. "Anyone that old who still likes to drive fancy cars is probably a good candidate for the computer age. Don't you think so?"

Leave it to Ashley to throw in her homegrown philosophy. In the short time I'd known her, she always managed to pick just the right time to insert her strange-but-true comments.

"Curiosity killed the cat, right?" she said, laughing.

"Excuse me?"

"Your curiosity got the best of you," she began to summarize. "So you nosied around in Miss Spindler's attic."

"Right."

"Merry, you really can't expect to be too surprised with the result, can you?"

"I'm not dead, am I?"

"No . . . no, that's not what the old proverb means." Once again, she tried to get me to see the light. "What you did—out of pure inquisitiveness, of course—was bound to get you into trouble in the long run."

"But I'm *not* in trouble," I insisted.

"Well, I think you might be if Miss Spindler ever finds out."

I proceeded to tell her about the old lady's email pals. "I guess you could say she wanted to be found out. Maybe she wanted us to know that she's a truly 'with it' old lady."

"She's cool, all right. And I'll be the first to congratulate her," Ashley said.

"Well, I don't know if that's such a good idea."

"Why not?"

"Because she doesn't realize that very many of us know yet."

Ashley's sigh came through to my end of the phone. Loud and long. "Now I'm completely confused."

"I don't blame you." I was dying to tell her that I wouldn't be playing the Alliteration Game anymore. (The thought was triggered by the *c* words she'd just used.) But I thought better of it and decided to keep that decision secret. Just between Jon Klein and me.

EIGHTEEN

Miss Spindler came for supper with bells on. She was all dolled up—a touch of lipstick and pinkish cheeks. She wore a long, floral broomstick skirt and a hot-pink blouse to match the rosebuds in her flowing skirt.

"Now, dearies, I brought along Parmesan cheese to sprinkle on the pasta and enough warm garlic bread to feed every last one of our Amish neighbors." She said this with a playful smile on her wrinkled face.

"You're getting to know lots of them?" I blurted without thinking.

"Who's that, dear?" she asked.

"Our Amish neighbors," I repeated.

Skip was trying not to explode in the corner of the kitchen between the wall and Mom's African violet plants. I could tell by the way he was smashing his lips together—and that silly grin on his face. Man, was I crazy to bring this up, or what?

"As a matter of fact, I *have* been getting myself acquainted with a whole bunch of Plain folk, come to think of it," she said.

"Oh?" I had to play dumb. I wasn't supposed to know this.

"I'm sure your nice young man—that Jonathan Klein, was it?—told you all about my little chat with him yesterday afternoon." Her beady eyes were on me now. I had a mighty powerful feeling that there was no way out. I had to fess up.

"Well, first of all"—I said this for Skip's sake—"Jon's not my nice young man. I don't mean that he's *not* nice, just not mine. At least, not yet." I was sliding deeper and deeper, right to where Skip was most interested, no doubt.

She ignored the explanation and placed the casserole dish on the table. Then she called my brother over. "The food's hot, but not for long. We'd best get started."

After the prayer, I asked if I could start again. "Please do," Skip had the gall to say. Grinning, no less.

Sighing, I decided to back up to the real point of Miss Spindler's earlier comment. "I was very surprised to hear about your email friends," I began. "And, yes, Jonathan did fill me in on that."

A beautiful smile, pure and sweet, spread across her face. "Ah, Merry, dearie, I'm ever so glad to have dreamed up such a right fine name for my little attic office," she said. "It's *Windows on the Hill*, you know."

I knew but didn't dare let on.

"My, oh my, I've met a good many folk on the Web."

I had to work hard at chewing my food—keeping it in my mouth—and not spraying it across the table. But the laugh insisted, and I grabbed for my napkin.

Miss Spindler looked worried. "What is it, Merry?"

I was shaking my head, patting my chest. "I'm all right, really I am."

Now she had the most peculiar look on her face. Like she thought she must've said something quite comical. "Well, I daresay my sense of humor must surely be improving."

I was nodding, eyeballing Skip. He started nodding his head, too. We talked awhile longer about computers and how easy it was to link up unknowingly with weirdos and unlikely strangers. People who might not be good for us. Miss Spindler agreed and said that she was being careful of that.

During dessert, Skip brought up the subject of Abednego. "Did he ever show up?"

I slouched sadly. "Don't get me started. Honestly, I thought I'd never give up on him, but I have to admit I'm starting to wonder if God had other plans for my old cat."

Skip's eyebrows rose, and he pursed his lips. "He was always such a crafty creature."

"*Was?* Don't say it that way. It sounds like you think he's already dead."

"Hold on, now, Merry," Miss Spindler was saying, reaching over and patting my hand. "We just don't know yet, now, do we?"

"He's been missing for six days—unbearable days.

129

Cats always come home after a storm, don't they?"

Miss Spindler was quiet for a moment. "They do, I suppose, unless someone comes along and claims them for their own."

I sat up in my chair. "Do you really think someone stole my Abednego?"

Skip leaned his head into his hands and rubbed his face, while Miss Spindler tried to calm me down. "Wouldn't that be far better than finding out the poor little thing had up and died?"

I thought about that. Miss Old Hawk Eyes Spindler was right. Still, I found it terribly confusing when she insisted that I come right home with her after supper dishes were finished. "Let's talk some more about that lost cat of yours," she said.

As I walked with our quirky old neighbor across the backyard and up the slope of her own property—all that time—I could see my brother's ridiculous smile in my mind.

NINETEEN

"You sit here, dearie." Miss Spindler stepped aside so I faced her computer screen directly.

"Where will *you* sit?" I asked.

She was already one step ahead of me, pulling a folding chair across the attic's carpeted floor. "Here we are," she said.

She asked me to click onto her email program, which I did. "Now," she said, "I was hoping you'd read each of this week's messages to me."

This week's. There were thirty messages!

"Oh, I have such a hard time," she explained, taking off her thick glasses and showing me where the trifocal line began. "You have no idea just how difficult it is to see the words."

"Maybe you should order a software program with larger letters." I'd heard of such things, especially for folks who suffered from partial blindness.

"Well, for now, I've got *you* here," she said. "Thank you for agreeing to help this old lady."

I began to read her personal messages, feeling a bit awkward. The first was from an Amish woman who said she lived just north of the Davises on SummerHill Lane. She described her busy day—washing and hanging out the clothes to dry, baking, cleaning, sewing, and gardening. On and on.

The writer signed off with: *Nobody's seen hide nor hair of a big black cat.*

"You asked her about Abednego?" I said, turning to face Miss Spindler.

"Oh yes, I've asked every one of my email friends."

"Is that why you wanted me to come help you?"

She responded with a quick smile. "Keep on reading," she said, moving her hands.

I read the next five, but none of the writers had seen my cat. We were clear down to the next to the last message. An Amish lady two houses down from the Fishers' place—out near the highway—wrote to say that she'd spotted a large animal prowling around her house.

If it's a house cat, it's a very big one, she wrote. *I daresay that one would take a batch of field mice to keep full.*

"Sounds like Abednego!" I said, eager to read on.

Last night, we put out a bowl of milk for him. Fast as a wink, he drank it down. My grandson put out another bowl, and that one was gone in nothing flat. If ya wanna come and see for yourself about this here mouse-catcher, I'll hang on to him for ya, just a bit.

I was clapping my hands. "Can we go, Miss Spindler? Please?"

"It's getting late," she said, reminding me that Amish folk head for bed about eight-thirty. "I'll tell you what, dearie, we'll drive on over there. If the oil lamps are burnin' in the kitchen, we'll know they're still up."

Thrilled beyond belief, I closed down the Windows on the Hill. Miss Spindler was truly amazing.

❧   ❧

"Don't get your hopes up too high, dearie," she told me as we rode down SummerHill Lane.

Crickets were chirping to beat the band, and the moon was just starting to rise in the east. I sat in the front seat of the fanciest sports car this side of the Susquehanna River, praying that Abednego would be waiting on the front porch for us.

Miss Spindler pulled slowly into the driveway when we found the house. "See any lights?" I whispered.

"Not a one," she said.

I opened the car door. "I'm gonna go look for him."

"No . . . no, you mustn't be impatient, now. All good things come to those who wait."

I argued. "But I've been waiting nearly a week. Can't I at least walk around the house and call for him?"

She shook her head. "Not on your life, dearie. That's trespassing, pure and simple."

"I know, but—"

"No buts. We'll come back tomorrow."

"Abednego might be gone by then," I insisted.

"Not if these good folk are feeding him milk every day, he won't."

She had a point. Still, I wanted Abednego in my arms tonight!

"Here, kitty, kitty," I called softly. "It's Merry come to get you, baby. Come on, now, you know your Merry's here."

Miss Spindler was beside herself. "Get in the car," she said. "We best be goin'."

"I promise not to trespass," I said, moving to the front of the car. "It's Merry . . . Merry's here. Come on, little boy, you know you wanna go home."

The sky was dotted with shimmering silver flecks of light. All around me I heard the sounds of nightfall.

"You want some Kitty Kisses?" I said softly. "Merry's gonna give her little boy some treats."

I waited some more, listening for the slightest clue. The tiniest sound of a cat.

"Psst, Merry," called Miss Spindler. "We'll try again tomorrow." She flicked her headlights on and turned on the ignition.

Just then a light came on in the back of the house. "Look!" I said. "Someone's up." My heart was thumping with anticipation.

Miss Spindler was out of the car, catching up with me as I hurried around to the back door of the farmhouse. "Best let me handle this," she said, opening the screen door and knocking on the inside door.

"Jah, who's there?" said an Amishman, peering out at us.

"It's Ruby Spindler, your wife's friend up the road a piece. She wrote something about finding a stray cat."

The man was nodding his head, his gray beard bumping his chest each time he did. "Jah, we know of such a cat."

"He's here?" I asked excitedly. "Abednego's here?"

Looking quite perplexed, the man frowned and shook his head. "I never heard of that name—not for a cat."

"But it's him, isn't it?" I could hardly stand there, aching to know if they had him or not.

"Ach, I think ya must be mistaken. We saw no such tag on the cat—not nowhere." The man was beginning to close the door.

"Please," I said, "may I have a look at the cat you found?"

He paused, as if he wasn't sure he should invite us in or not.

Then behind me I heard a stirring in the bushes, followed by *meow*.

"Wait! I'd know that sound anywhere," I said, turning and scooping up my beloved baby into my arms. "Oh, you're safe, Abednego! You're truly safe."

I heard Miss Spindler thank the man.

"Well, that takes care of that," he said, closing the back door.

All the way home, I cuddled my cat. "Hey, I think you're fatter than before," I told him.

Abednego didn't talk back; instead, he purred like a motorboat and leaned his head against my arm.

"How can I ever thank you, Miss Spindler?" I asked.

She kept driving, probably deciding what she ought to say to me. Then it came. The cutest thing I'd heard all year. "Guess Old Hawk Eyes ain't so awful bad, now, is she?"

I sucked in a little breath, shocked that she knew her nickname. "I won't ask where you heard that," I said, snickering. "It's really none of my business, is it?"

Her head went back with hearty laughter. And I snuggled with my newly found pet.

It was a night to remember.

TWENTY

Miss Spindler was kind enough to let me take pictures of her attic computer room so I could show all my girl friends. And my new boyfriend. That's right, Jon Klein and I are "going out"—which means he calls me sometimes and we do things together at our church youth group. Stuff like that. But it's a dream come true, and I only wish Faithie were alive to witness my joy.

I haven't written Levi about it yet. I figure I can wait till he comes home this summer. Besides, he should feel relieved to hear the news, especially if he has someone new himself.

Dad and Mom are back from Costa Rica, and all they talk about is taking Skip and me the next time. "You'd love the people," Dad says. "They're so hungry for Jesus."

Speaking of hunger, Abednego has never been so interested in his regular kitty food. He learned a hard lesson by running away. But now that he's back home, his behavior is improving. Even Skip has noticed how placid and cooperative my wayward cat is now.

As for Chelsea, she's completely well and back to school. She says she's sorry she missed the day Jon and I sat together on the bus. She said she'd give anything to have been there. Of course, he and I still sit together, but Chelsea's right there, too. Either in front of us or right across the aisle.

The Alliteration Word Game is history—a thing of the past—for Jon and me, at least. Chelsea, Ashley, and Lissa are still going strong, and occasionally Miss Spindler tries her hand at alliterating. Jon and I are much better communicators without the limitation of having to match up every sentence and every group of words. I must admit, I've never been so happy.

Rachel Zook and I *finally* talked Miss Spindler into taking one of the gray kittens as a pet. When the light is just right, the sweet little thing matches Old Hawk Eyes' blue-gray hair!

Most of all, I'm thankful that God's eyes were on Abednego during those six worry-filled days. And I know something else: He used Old Hawk Eyes' curiosity and turned it into something good.

I'm thinking it might be time for a new nickname for my neighbor. Or maybe none at all.

FROM BEVERLY ... TO YOU

❧   ❧

I'm delighted that you're reading SUMMERHILL SECRETS. Merry Hanson is such a fascinating character—I can't begin to count the times I laughed while writing her humorous scenes. And I must admit, I always cry with her.

Not so long ago, I was Merry's age, growing up in Lancaster County, the home of the Pennsylvania Dutch—my birthplace. My grandma Buchwalter was Mennonite, as were many of my mother's aunts, uncles, and cousins. Some of my school friends were also Mennonite, so my interest and appreciation for the "plain" folk began early.

It is they, the Mennonite and Amish people—farmers, carpenters, blacksmiths, shopkeepers, quiltmakers, teachers, schoolchildren, and bed and breakfast owners—who best assisted me with the research for this series. Even though I have kept their identity private, I am thankful for these wonderfully honest and helpful friends.

If you want to learn more about Rachel Zook and her people, ask for my Amish bibliography when you write. I'll send you the book list along with my latest newsletter. Please include a *self-addressed, stamped envelope* for all correspondence. Thanks!

Beverly Lewis
%Bethany House Publishers
11400 Hampshire Ave. S.
Minneapolis, MN 55438

Also by Beverly Lewis

PICTURE BOOKS

Annika's Secret Wish   Cows in the House
Just Like Mama

THE CUL-DE-SAC KIDS
Children's Fiction

The Double Dabble Surprise	Tarantula Toes
The Chicken Pox Panic	Green Gravy
The Crazy Christmas Angel Mystery	Backyard Bandit Mystery
No Grown-ups Allowed	Tree House Trouble
Frog Power	The Creepy Sleep-Over
The Mystery of Case D. Luc	The Great TV Turn-Off
The Stinky Sneakers Mystery	Piggy Party
Pickle Pizza	The Granny Game
Mailbox Mania	Mystery Mutt
The Mudhole Mystery	Big Bad Beans
Fiddlesticks	The Upside-Down Day
The Crabby Cat Caper	The Midnight Mystery

ABRAM'S DAUGHTERS
Adult Fiction

The Covenant   The Betrayal
The Sacrifice

THE HERITAGE OF LANCASTER COUNTY
Adult Fiction

The Shunning   The Confession
The Reckoning

OTHER ADULT FICTION

The Postcard

The Crossroad

The Redemption of Sarah Cain

October Song

Sanctuary*

The Sunroom

www.BeverlyLewis.com

*with David Lewis

Early Teen Fiction Series From
Bethany House Publishers
(Ages 11–14)

———⊗∞⊗———

HIGH HURDLES • by Lauraine Snelling
Show jumper DJ Randall strives to defy the odds and achieve her dream of winning Olympic Gold.

HOLLY'S HEART • by Beverly Lewis
About to turn thirteen, Holly Meredith relies on her faith to help her through the challenges of family, school, friendships, and boys.

JANETTE OKE CLASSICS FOR GIRLS • by Janette Oke
Turn-of-the-century stories capture readers' hearts as they get to know teen girls facing the timeless challenges of growing up into Christlike young women.

SUMMERHILL SECRETS • by Beverly Lewis
Fun-loving Merry Hanson encounters mystery and excitement in Pennsylvania's Amish country.